THE
WRITER

A San Juan Islands Mystery
Book One

By
D.W. ULSTERMAN

This is a work of fiction.

The San Juan Islands Mysteries

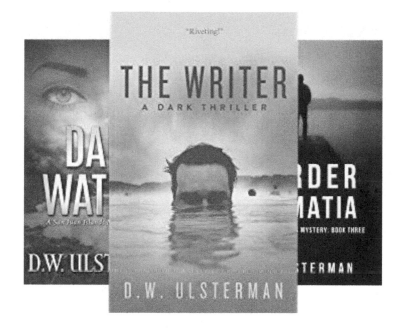

The Writer
Dark Waters
Murder on Matia
Rosario's Revenge
Roche Harbor Rogue
Turn Point Massacre
Deadman Island
The Truthing Tree
The Book of Bloodbone

To my dad.

He introduced me to the San Juan Islands.

A place that always made me feel as if I belonged.

Man is least himself when he talks in his own person.

Give him a mask, and he will tell you the truth.

-Oscar Wilde

PROLOGUE:

It's the humane thing to do…

Decklan Stone just recently turned ten years old when his father Milton gave him a very hard lesson in compassion.

There were seven kittens born a week earlier that Decklan's father decided, in very serious and determined tones, needed to be drowned in the small pond located in the very back portion of the Stone family property.

"This is the right thing to do, Decklan. We can't have all these cats running around here. They'll starve, suffer, and then die. The world doesn't want them so it's our job to get rid of what the world has no use for. Go into the garden shed and bring me one of those burlap sacks we used for the potato sack races on your birthday."

Milton Stone was an educator—a high school teacher of English literature.

In private, though he would never admit it, Milton was also a devoted sadist. Few things in life gave him greater pleasure than to see others suffering, both physically and emotionally. When his son exclaimed happily at the dinner table the previous night that he had discovered where a semi-feral neighborhood cat had given birth to a litter of kittens, Decklan's father recognized another such opportunity to indulge his dark nature.

With every tear shed by his son, Milton's pleasure increased exponentially, though it was well hidden beneath a layer of carefully crafted, fatherly wisdom.

"Decklan, it's the *humane* thing to do."

Ten-year-old Decklan had no idea what the word humane meant, and in that moment he didn't care to find out. All he knew was that it was associated with the impending murder of seven innocent lives.

"Decklan, stop your crying! Come here and hold the sack open."

Milton's son did as he was told. He knew better than to question his father's authority, believing that to do so might very well result in his being thrown into the pond along with the kittens.

The sky was overcast, the upstate New York air thick with unusually high humidity. The lush, well-manicured grass of the Stone family's backyard had often been an escapist oasis for young Decklan, but on this day, it was to be the scene of a most horrific crime.

Milton Stone held several small rocks taken from the side of the yard and proceeded to dump them into the sack held by his young, teary-eyed son.

"Now show me where the kittens are."

Decklan hesitated, thinking he might yet convince his normally all-knowing father that he couldn't remember.

Milton's voice issued the familiar warning growl that signaled he was nearing dangerous levels of displeasure. His long, lean and clean-shaven face was marked by a disapproving frown. The blue eyes that resided behind a pair of thick prescription glasses narrowed slightly, communicating how close Decklan was to his father's reactive precipice.

"Decklan, TAKE ME TO THE KITTENS."

The boy's eyes glared back defiantly.

He refused his father's request.

Retribution was swiftly delivered in the form of a firm slap across Decklan's cheek. He was struck with enough force that he fell to the ground.

"Don't make me ask you again."

Decklan stood up far more quickly than the father would have thought possible. He straightened his shoulders and jutted his chin upward while he ignored the stinging pain that permeated the side of his face.

The gesture left Milton momentarily stunned. Decklan had never been so impudent before.

"Very well, I'll just find them myself and you won't have a chance to tell them good-bye. I'm disappointed in you, Decklan. I wouldn't have thought you to be such a cruel little monster."

Milton could barely conceal his smile as he watched his son struggle with abandoning the kittens in their moment of greatest need. There was just a short pause before Decklan relented, emotionally spent and still physically hurt.

He pointed to the shed.

"They're in the back in a hole under the floor."

Decklan watched as Milton gave him a wide, approving smile and noted how his father's eyes remained devoid of any warmth or kindness. The elder Stone's eyes never smiled.

Never.

"Very good, Decklan. Come on then, let's get to it."

Father and son walked across the yard's thick, green grass and then made their way to the back of the shed. Decklan could hear the kittens meowing loudly for their mother who had seemingly gone missing.

"Reach into the hole and grab a kitten and put it into the sack."

Decklan's tears streaked his face and his nose began to run, causing him to sniffle loudly. Milton reached out with and pushed against the boy's back.

"Son, don't disappoint me. I told you. This is the humane thing to do."

Decklan reached into the hole underneath the shed with trembling hands and withdrew the first of seven kittens. Each one had eyes that had just recently opened. Their soft fur smelled of shared warmth, and dirt. Decklan had already named each kitten and proceeded to recite those names silently as he dropped them one by one into the sack.

Furry Ear, White Sock, Stubby, Big Nose, Pink Toes, Long Tail, Chub-Chub.

Milton Stone closed the sack filled with kittens and rocks. He nodded at his son and again gave his unsmiling smile.

"Now we go to the pond."

During the journey to the back of the yard the kittens began to wail loudly at their dislocation and Decklan watched in horror as the sack's exterior showed the newborn feline siblings moving frantically from inside their burlap tomb.

I'm not going to cry any more. I won't let him make me cry.

The slow march to the pond was nearly unbearable for Decklan. His eyes remained fixed upon the sack being dragged across the grass by his father while his ears were assaulted by the kittens' plaintive cries to be returned to the warm and safe confines of their former home underneath the shed.

Decklan began quietly humming a song that had recently been repeatedly playing on the small, portable radio he received as a birthday gift. It was a habit he employed during times of great stress. As a younger child he'd often hum a commercial jingle. On this day, as the kittens' collective panic intensified the closer the bag came to the awaiting pond, it was David Bowie's "Space Oddity" that played on a loop inside of the boy's increasingly dismayed mind.

When his father stopped in front of the pond and looked down at his son and began to speak, Decklan only heard the soft strumming of an acoustic guitar and David Bowie's voice in his head—calm, comforting, and otherworldly.

Milton Stone lifted the sack off the ground, swung it around his head, and then flung it with a loud grunt into the water.

Planet Earth is blue and there's nothing I can do, Bowie sang.

The music stopped the moment the bag hit the pond's surface. Decklan flinched and tried to look away, but found he was unable to do so. The burlap sack floated for a few agonizing seconds, an intolerable length of time that allowed Decklan to make out the unmistakable outline of tiny paws pushing against the thick fabric as the kittens fought to be free.

They wanted so badly to live.

Milton Stone relished the strain evident on his son's face as the bag slipped silently beneath the dark cover of water. He reached out and gently placed his hand around Decklan's shoulders. It wasn't enough to simply see the boy's pain. The schoolteacher had to *feel* it as well. When Milton spoke next, his voice conveyed an unusually cheerful demeanor that was oddly juxtaposed with the seven bodies that lay at the bottom of the pond.

"And that takes care of that!"

Decklan's father turned and began to walk away. After a few steps he paused but kept his back to his son.

"You did the right thing, Decklan. You did the *humane* thing. Don't forget that."

For the remainder of his childhood, Decklan Stone never did forget that day, especially the haunting movements and sounds living things make as they drown.

His nightmares wouldn't allow it.

1.

Late spring:

The water was especially calm during twenty-two-year-old Adele Plank's quarter-mile voyage from Deer Harbor to the private island of her interview subject for the college newspaper assignment she hoped might lead to her much-desired future as a journalist. She had first read Decklan Stone's one and only bestseller, *Manitoba*, shortly after her sixteenth birthday. It had been a gift from her now deceased grandmother Beatrice, who declared the story, "one of the best I ever read!" Grandma Beatrice read a *lot* of books, so Adele knew the compliment likely had at least some merit.

It had taken Adele less than two days to finish the three-hundred-and-seventy-page novel, a feat which she had since never bested. She read it for a second time, and then a third, memorizing the subtle nuances of each character, especially the way the writer weaved multiple plot lines into a remarkably satisfying conclusion.

She loved *Manitoba* and so, by default, she came to love and admire its author as well.

"You know, it's been a long time since I've taken someone besides myself to Mr. Stone's island. I think maybe, heck, almost four years and that was his publicist who flew all the way here from New York for a meeting that lasted all of an hour. I remember him telling me Mr. Stone hates the telephone, doesn't do email, none of that stuff. With him it's in person or it's not at all. Anyway, that's what we all call it around here, Stone's Island, but its real name is Fawn Island. That's what I knew it as when I was a little kid, but he's been living there for thirty-odd years now, so we all just call it Stone's Island these days."

Adele gave a polite nod and half-smile to the somewhat incoherent, mile-a-minute ramblings of the man who had earlier introduced himself to her in an oddly childlike voice, as Will Speaks. The forty-six-year-old Deer Harbor local had a ruddy complexion, ample belly, and a wide, smiling face that complimented his seemingly good-natured demeanor. Will had been the one contacted by Adele's newspaper editor to transport her across Deer Harbor on his small Boston Whaler skiff. Even as she watched the passing water playfully splash against the little boat's dull, white hull, she still couldn't believe she was actually going to meet the man who had given life to *Manitoba*.

Her newspaper editor had called Adele into his cramped and paper-strewn office just three days earlier to give her the good news that Decklan Stone's longtime publicist had contacted them to say the author agreed to the one-on-one interview Adele had proposed weeks earlier.

"I don't know why he chose you, Ms. Plank, but he did. Stone hasn't spoken to anyone in the media since his wife's death and that was more than twenty-five years ago. This interview is going to get you national attention. You might have just been given the journalist's version of the winning lottery ticket."

It was that reclusive nature that had enhanced Decklan Stone's appeal to Adele since her first reading of *Manitoba*. Stone's reputation as a mysterious recluse gave him an aura of the unknown that fascinated Adele. She had spent hours staring at his black-and-white photo that dominated *Manitoba's* interior back cover. She knew the faint lines that crossed his forehead, the large, expressive eyes, the slightly upturned nose, and the full-lipped, almost feminine mouth that contrasted his strong, undeniably masculine jawline. She could also recall nearly every strand of the unruly, dark hair that crowned the head of the man that she, and many others, considered a literary genius.

"Have you ever seen him?"

Will turned around in the wooden seat that barely contained his large and lumpy frame so he could look behind him where Adele sat on the single wood bench at the very back of the Whaler.

"Who, the writer?"

Adele nodded.

"Yeah, I guess I have, though not for a while and it wasn't up close. Late last summer after dropping off his monthly supply order I looked back on my way back to Deer Harbor and saw him standing on the dock staring at me. I waved at him. He didn't wave back."

This bit of information piqued Adele's interest. For the first time since stepping onto his boat, she wanted to hear what Will Speaks had to say.

"What did he look like?"

Will shrugged his wide shoulders, making certain to talk loud enough so his voice could be heard above the droning din of the small two-stroke outboard motor.

"Oh, I don't know. Kind of thin, tall, I think he was wearing a sweatshirt. There was almost fifty yards of water between us by then. Like I said, I waved, but he didn't wave back. Makes me think he's probably as much of a jerk as some folks say."

Adele was quick to ask a follow up question.

"People around here don't like him?"

Will, possibly sensing the verbal trap, quickly shook his head.

"I didn't say *that*. I guess it's more, well, we don't really *know* him. He's a mystery. I mean, that's why you're coming out here to do the talking thing, right? So you can try and solve the big mystery of the writer?"

Adele wasn't about to let Will off the hook that easy. She also made note of his phrase, "the talking thing" thinking it something a much younger person would say.

"But you just said some around here say he's a jerk. Those were *your* words, Mr. Speaks. I'd appreciate knowing who those people are."

Will winced as he realized he should have kept his mouth shut. His next reply was again sprinkled with an oddly childlike speech pattern juxtaposed within the body of a full-grown man.

"Oh, I didn't mean people *today*. I'm sure your, uh, research, if you've done research, you know about his wife's death, her disappearance and all that stuff. There were some around here who thought maybe it wasn't like the cops said it was, is all I meant. I was just a kid then, so don't take what I say as how it is, or something."

Adele knew the story well. Decklan Stone's young, beautiful wife was reported lost in a nighttime boating accident, her body never recovered. That tragedy took place just three years after Stone had become among the most successful and widely regarded authors of his day when he was but twenty-seven years old. He was thirty when Calista Stone was said to have slipped beneath the cold and dark, San Juan Islands waters never to return, and from then on, whatever continued literary promise Decklan Stone might have had, seemingly perished along with his wife. He had become an extension of the tragic romance that was such a critical element within *Manitoba,* a condition that no doubt contributed to the novel's return to the bestseller list immediately following Calista Stone's death and the mystery surrounding it, thus earning Decklan that much more money, mystery, and notoriety.

Few things are as attractive or profitable as human tragedy.

"Didn't your father used to be the San Juan County Sheriff?"

Will's eyes widened slightly, a gesture that let Adele know her earlier research was correct. He gently increased the Whaler's speed, seemingly wanting to be rid of the college girl and her questions.

"Yeah."

"Is he one of those you just said doesn't like Decklan Stone?"

Will turned away from Adele and pointed to the private dock that extended like a long, rigid finger from a small, densely wooded island near the entrance to Deer Harbor.

"We're just about there, Ms. Plank. I'll be pulling in portside."

Adele had no idea what portside was until after the Whaler turned to the right to allow its left side to come to a slow and well controlled stop directly against the dock. Will tied off the skiff, jumped onto the dock, and extended his hand to help Adele from the boat.

"Is that the same boat?"

The boat in question was a forty-one foot, red, white and blue, wooden-hulled Chris Craft. Adele had seen photos of it while scanning the Internet for information pertaining to Calista Stone's death. She knew the boat to have been built in 1961 and purchased by Decklan and Calista shortly after they bought Fawn Island in 1986, following the bestselling success of *Manitoba*.

Will scowled as he tried to avoid Adele's eyes. His response was a barely audible grumble. He appeared not to want to look at the boat any more than he wanted to look directly at Adele.

"Yes, it's the same boat. He has Old Jack come out every six months to keep her looking right."

Adele had no idea who Old Jack was but made a mental note to follow up on the name. She then took out her phone and snapped several pictures of the boat, the dock, and the hillside. It was an undeniably beautiful place, with rock-strewn beaches, abrupt, dark- stoned cliffs, and majestic evergreen trees that rose up like towering, silent sentinels that kept watch over the small island.

"The path begins at the end of the dock. It'll take you to the house. If I remember right, it gets a bit steep, but a young, pretty woman like you should have no trouble at all."

Again, Adele noticed how Will would sometimes use a word or expression that didn't quite fit with how a man his age would normally talk.

Not sure what his thinking I'm pretty has anything to do with my being able to get up the hill.

Adele readjusted her backpack and then offered her hand which Will quickly took in his much larger and calloused one.

"Thank you for helping to get me here, Mr. Speaks. I hope to have a chance to speak with you again soon."

Will gave Adele a forced smile and shrugged.

"I can't make any promises about that. I don't want to cause any trouble with Mr. Stone. He pays me good to bring him his supplies and jobs like this aren't exactly easy to come by around here. Oh, when you call me to say you're ready to be picked up, you might have to use Mr. Stone's regular, uh, the old kind of phone. Cell phones don't always work out here."

Adele smiled and then readjusted her backpack again, realizing she was doing so more out of nervousness than necessity.

"Okay, I'll do that. It shouldn't be more than a few hours."

After she took several steps on the dock toward the awaiting trail to Decklan Stone's home overlooking the waters that surrounded his private island, Adele heard Will call out to her.

"You be careful, Ms. Plank."

Adele tried to reassure him with a smile.

"I'll take my time getting up there. Don't worry. I won't slip."

The smile normally affixed to Will's face vanished. His eyes narrowed as he gave Adele a long, hard stare.

"I'm not talking about you getting up to the house. I'm talking about you getting back."

It was at that moment Adele wondered why the seemingly affable, albeit childlike, Will Speaks wasn't escorting her to the writer's home that was almost entirely hidden behind a wall of trees.

"Have you been to the house, Mr. Speaks?"

Will shook his head.

"No, not for a long time."

"Why not?"

Will peered up at the faint outline of the Stone residence through a gap in the tree line.

"Mr. Stone doesn't allow it. He's made that clear. I drop off the supplies on the dock, and then leave. At the end of the month a check is mailed to my dad from a place in New York with a list of supplies to be delivered the next month. That's what my dad tells me to do and so, uh, so that's what I do."

"And why do you think I need to be careful when I get up there?"

Will looked down as he shuffled his feet, appearing even more like a nervous child than a grown man. He felt as if he was being watched from above.

"It's just that I think people who meet someone who they think they know are kind of let down. And you're not the first fan of the writer to come around here hoping to get a peek. I figure everyone just needs to let things be. Let him live up there alone because that's what he seems to want, and I think people should get what they want."

Adele readjusted her backpack yet again.

"Yeah, but I'm the first one who he actually invited, right?"

Will gave Adele a slow nod as he kept his eyes locked onto hers.

"I guess so. Unless I hear different, expect me back here in three hours like you said."

Adele was both fascinated and just a bit uncomfortable at Will's sudden concern for her well-being. She quickly pushed aside her discomfort when she remembered she was about to meet the reclusive Decklan Stone—*in person*.

"Okay, Mr. Speaks, and thank you again."

She gave Will a quick wave as he hopped back onto the Whaler, restarted its motor, and began to move away from the dock.

He didn't wave back.

2.

The path at the end of the dock consisted of a narrow trail of compacted gravel that led upward and then through a dense area of trees. After several steps, Adele paused to look behind her at the glistening, glasslike waters below. She could see Will navigating the Whaler back to the Deer Harbor marina and then she moved her eyes upward to follow the slow, circling path of a bald eagle. Between a gap in the trees she saw a small cove almost entirely hidden from the main body of water by a dark, circular outcrop of rock. Behind that was a small, red-hulled fiberglass runabout tied by a long rope around the trunk of a tree that hung over a sand and pebble beach.

Adele took a deep breath and relished the intoxicating mixture of saltwater and trees.

It was certainly a beautiful place, the kind of place she could easily imagine a writer like Decklan Stone living out his days in quiet solitude.

I would love to live here.

Adele was a student at the nearby university in Bellingham, some twenty-six nautical miles from Deer Harbor, but she had grown up in Washington State's interior. She was born and raised in the small town of Concrete in Skagit County.

She had never been to the San Juan Islands, though, she knew of people who summered there and spoke glowingly of its enchanting and mysterious nature. Over four hundred smaller, but no less beautiful, islands, accompanied the primary islands of San Juan, Orcas and Lopez. It was a boater's paradise, a place that had long attracted visitors from all over the world.

"Hello there."

Adele whirled around and found herself staring up at Decklan Stone. Her eyes widened and her mouth fell partly open as she tried in vain to think of something to say.

"Can I take your backpack? The trail gets a bit steep, though it does make for a nice workout."

Oh, my, Adele thought. *He's gorgeous!*

Decklan appeared remarkably well-preserved. Though Adele knew him to be fifty-seven years of age, he could easily have passed for a man in his early forties. His lightly bearded face was nearly devoid of lines, his blue eyes bright and clear, and his dark hair nearly as thick and unruly as the black-and-white photo of him that accompanied Adele's copy of *Manitoba*, taken thirty years ago.

Adele was horrified to find her mouth barely able to form words.

"Oh, yes, uh, thank you. Hello, my name is Adele, Adele Plank."

The author quickly dissected the distance between them in a few confident steps down the trail, bringing with him the subtle scent of cologne and tobacco. His voice was low, smooth, and enticing. He was just over six-feet tall, with wide shoulders, narrow hips, and especially long, athletic legs housed in tan khakis that accompanied a thick, cream-colored wool sweater. A pair of dark grey, loafer-style boating shoes adorned his feet.

"Yes, I know who you are, Ms. Plank. I invited you."

Adele tried not to blush but failed as she placed her backpack into Decklan's long-fingered, outstretched hands. She made note of the gold flash of a classic Rolex watch as it peeked out from underneath the sleeve of his sweater.

"How was the journey here?"

Adele cleared her throat and smiled.

"Oh, it was great. It's such a beautiful place. And this island! It's just…it's just perfect."

Decklan stood staring down at Adele for a few uncomfortable seconds, and then he looked up at the trees as his voice took on a contemplative tone.

"Perfect? I don't know about that, but it *is* home."

The author shook off whatever memories had suddenly taken him away and he smiled again, flashing a row of brilliant white and perfectly aligned teeth.

"Just follow me then, and we'll be to the house in no time."

Adele did as she was told, struggling just a bit to keep up with the longer-legged writer as he easily made his way up the narrow, steepening path.

With her lungs stinging their angry discontent, Adele looked across a small, grass and flower clearing at a log-framed structure that loomed on the other side and was stunned to find that it appeared exactly as it did from the decades ago news clippings. The two-story home had a covered, wrap-around front porch that dominated the entrance, and a large balcony that led out via a pair of French doors from what was the second-floor master bedroom above.

It was quite literally the house *Manitoba*'s long-ago success had built.

"Wow."

Decklan turned around and looked at the visibly awe-struck college newspaper reporter behind him.

"It's just wood and concrete with a washed-up writer hiding out inside of it."

Adele snorted far louder than she would have liked.

"I think it's a lot more than *that*, Mr. Stone."

"Please, just call me Decklan. Mr. Stone sounds so…old."

Adele shook her head with enough force that it made her cheeks jiggle.

"You don't look old. You don't look old *at all*."

Adele was mortified at her behavior. She had rehearsed this moment a hundred times in her head and yet she was doing exactly what she had promised she wouldn't—come off as some star-struck fan.

Decklan chuckled, both surprised and grateful for Adele's overly enthusiastic defense of his allegedly not-yet-old, appearance.

"Well thank you. I'm more than vain enough to admit I enjoy knowing someone your age sees me as something other than a decrepit relic of some bygone era. Let's go inside. Would you like some tea?"

Adele nodded while silently reminding herself to calm the hell down while also in shock that she was about to have tea with Decklan Stone inside his home.

Oh. My. God.

Decklan stepped up onto the porch and then pushed open the custom-made, dark-wood-stained front door. He looked down at Adele and gave her a reassuring wink.

"Here we are, Ms. Plank. Welcome to my home."

The interior of the Stone residence was as tasteful as its exterior. The handcrafted furnishings were sparse, simple, and yet they exuded quality and class. The floors were wide, reddish planks that softly creaked and groaned when walked upon. Decklan tapped his foot lightly against the wood.

"The floors came from a decommissioned wood-hulled trans-Pacific sailboat from the late-eighteenth century, shipped here from Taiwan when the house was first built. I've always appreciated the idea of something old finding a new purpose, a kind of immortality."

Adele wanted to sigh but made certain she didn't. She had never heard anyone say anything quite like that, and it left her feeling like the luckiest person alive to have heard it spoken in the wonderfully soft yet masculine voice of Decklan Stone.

"Can I use that quote?"

Decklan's head tilted to the side as his brow arched upward.

"I'm sorry?"

"Uh, for the story, I'd like to use what you just said."

Decklan paused, and then his eyes widened as he seemingly remembered why Adele was there in the first place.

"Oh, of course. Yes, feel free to use what you want. I don't have any preconditions, though, my publicist has demanded approval of the final piece prior to publication."

Adele nodded quickly, not wanting to ruin the time with her literary-hero host with the more mundane, real-world talk of business.

"Yes, Mr. Stone. I mean Decklan."

Decklan flashed his brilliant smile again and motioned for Adele to follow him into the A-framed great room. Massive floor-to-ceiling windows offered sweeping views of the San Juan Islands and the surrounding waters.

"Have a seat and I'll be out with some tea in just a moment," Decklan said.

Adele stared through the windows and then scanned the room. A couch and two matching chairs faced the windows with a coffee table made entirely of driftwood. A large bookshelf dominated one wall. On the right was a massive stone fireplace, and next to it, a hallway into which Decklan disappeared. Adele assumed it led to the kitchen; she could hear water running. Aside from the couch and chairs, there were no other furnishings. Even the walls were absent of any artwork.

Everything about the room is intended to focus you on the view, and what a view it is.

Adele took out her phone and snapped a couple of pictures of the postcard-like scenery outside. She felt a slight breeze and looked up to see a large ceiling fan repeating a slow, circular path directly above her. The home smelled of Decklan Stone, his woodsy-leather cologne with just a trace of tobacco.

I'd love to wake up to that scent every morning.

"Oh, you're still standing! Please, have a seat, some tea, and let's see about getting this little interview of yours started, shall we? I hope you like white tea. My mother introduced it to me years ago and it has become something of a daily ritual."

Adele lowered herself into the chair to one side of the couch while Decklan, after handing her a teacup, did the same on the other side. He took a slow sip, savored it, and then lifted his eyes to his guest. Adele willed her hands to stop trembling as she brought the teacup to her lips.

The tea had a light, floral scent with a nearly undetectable hint of honey.

"Mmm, it's good," Adele said. "Thank you."

Decklan appeared pleased by the compliment. He took another sip from his own cup and then cleared his throat and shrugged.

"Well, shall we begin?"

Adele reached into her backpack and withdrew a small tape recorder, a gift from her mother when she was a little girl who dreamed of being a reporter. She preferred it instead to the more modern digital options because of its sentimental value. Decklan pointed to the device.

"It appears you value old things as well. I haven't seen one of those in years!"

Adele responded with a sheepish grin.

"Is it okay that I record our conversations?"

Decklan nodded while he swirled the contents of his cup.

"Of course. That's what reporters do, right?"

Adele opened her mouth to say something, but momentarily lost her train of thought. Her hands trembled again when she finally replied.

"To be honest, I don't really know. I've done a few stories for my college newspaper, but this is really something way beyond my experience. And the fact is I'm a big-big fan of yours."

Decklan folded his hands and placed them against his salt and pepper stubbled chin.

"I'm confident you'll do just fine, Ms. Plank. Please proceed. Perhaps we should start with the proverbial elephant in the room. Ask the question everyone wants to ask of me, the question that has been the primary reason for my retreating from the all-too-superficial world of literary celebrity."

Adele felt her eyes blinking rapidly as she fought a terrible panic rising up from within her. She had planned to avoid the subject of Calista Stone's death, at least initially.

But now he's demanding I start with it. Is he testing me? Could I end up being thrown out of here without an interview?

She took a slow, deep breath and stared into Decklan's eyes. They were reassuring, willing her to do what, just seconds earlier, she had no intention of doing. The words came out rushed, sounding pathetically amateurish to Adele's ears. She was instantly horrified at having spoken them.

"Did you kill your wife?"

Outside, the prehistoric squawk of a great blue heron flying over the island reverberated off the home's interior walls. Decklan's eyes narrowed as he leaned forward with his tightly folded hands still resting against his chin. From somewhere else in the home, Adele heard the faint ticking of a clock. Though he only paused for a moment it felt like an eternity to the young reporter. Decklan's voice was sad and distant—its tone wrapped tightly around the pain of some terrible regret.

"Yes, Ms. Plank, I believe I did."

3.

Sunlight broke through the massive great room windows and washed over a suddenly still and silent, Decklan Stone. It was then Adele saw the hints of age illuminated on his face, the lines that extended beyond the corners of his eyes, and the strands of grey that ran through the otherwise dark and unkempt hair atop his head. He might have been remarkably well preserved, but he was not entirely immune to the toll of time.

Adele was surprised by how much she had expected the author to say what he did. She didn't believe she had just been witness to an admission of outright murder, but rather a man's belief in his responsibility for his wife's tragic demise. The two sat staring at one another before Decklan finally held up his hand and shook his head.

"I'm sorry, that was too much. I know now we should not have started there. I apologize and hope I didn't make you too uncomfortable, but if you are, I certainly understand."

Adele straightened in her chair, determined to expand the parameters of the interview to include that which remained unspoken.

"Just the opposite, Decklan. Your instincts are right. It's the issue that has pretty much defined how people think of you and so perhaps it's also the issue that defines how you think of yourself. We *should* talk about it, though, if you want to wait until later, I'm okay with that."

Decklan's mouth extended into an almost-smile, while his gaze lifted toward the expansive view beyond the windows.

"Yes, I think perhaps it is best we wait to cross that rather unstable bridge. I promise to speak with you about it but just not right now."

Decklan continued to look at the waters and islands beyond his home as Adele proceeded with another question that was just slightly less pressing to her than the first.

"Why me?"

"I'm sorry?" he asked.

Adele waited for the author's gaze to return to her before answering. His head turned and he again regarded her with a slightly arched brow.

"Why did you choose *me* to for your first interview after so many years of silence? Why pick some college kid with hardly a resume to her name?"

Decklan's eyes softened as he folded his arms across his chest.

"Is that how you see yourself? As merely some naïve and inexperienced *college kid*?"

Adele did in fact wonder what Decklan Stone saw when he looked at her. She knew she was somewhat attractive, more cute than beautiful, though, she was unable to shed a nagging ten pounds she felt made her more "rounded" than she would like. Her medium length, brown hair was most often kept back in a ponytail. What little makeup she wore was both simple and subtle, and her attire, such as it was, rarely went beyond a comfortable pair of blue jeans and a sweatshirt.

High class she was not.

"I know I'm not really a reporter yet. You could have a New York or Los Angeles or Seattle reporter up here the next day if you told them you were going to grant an interview, right?"

Decklan shrugged. It was such a slight and simple gesture and yet it elicited a silent revelation from Adele.

He's elegant, she thought. *I've never thought of a man as elegant but that's what he is.*

"Perhaps they might after they get on that Internet thing and find out who I am, or rather, *who I was.*"

It was Adele's turn to shake her head.

"Don't sell yourself short. I looked up your author ranking. *Manitoba* still sells thousands of copies a year."

Decklan finished his tea and then set the cup down onto its saucer on the coffee table.

"Ah, I guess that explains why those royalty checks keep making their way to me."

"You haven't answered my question," Adele continued. "Why me?"

Decklan shifted his left leg over his right and pretended to straighten the crisp crease of his khakis as he considered the question.

"I liked your letter, the one you sent to my publicist requesting the interview. It was friendly without being pretentious, had a hint of the curious but not overly fawning, and most important, you sounded sincere. The older I get, the more I value sincerity. I would add the timing of your letter helped as well, it being thirty years since *Manitoba's* publication. I don't necessarily care for overtly maudlin reflection, but I'm not entirely immune to it, either."

Adele felt her heart pounding inside her chest. The interview was proceeding. Decklan Stone was talking, and she knew it was her job to keep him doing so.

"Why haven't you published anything since *Manitoba*?"

The tips of the author's fingers lightly massaged his temple. His lips pursed and then he refolded his arms over his chest.

"I guess it's because I didn't feel I had anything left in me to say after Calista's death, at least not anything of value. I could have faked it like so many other writers do, but that would have been a betrayal of her, and I had already betrayed her enough. She was a big part of *Manitoba's* success, you know. She pushed me to continue working on it, revising it, and then to have the courage to put it out there in the hopes someone would be willing to publish it.

"Manitoba was my story, but we wrote it together. When it was turned down the first time, she told me to keep trying. Then it was turned down for a second time, and a third, and yet her belief in me and the story *never* diminished. Not even a little. She was more than I deserved."

"Why do you think that?"

Decklan's eyes lowered slightly.

"You've researched me, my history and reputation when I was a younger man?"

Adele nodded.

"You were greatly admired following *Manitoba's* success. That must have been a lot of pressure for someone still so young. You loved your wife, but you loved other women as well?"

For the first time since they met, Adele detected a hint of anger in Decklan's voice.

"NO, I never loved anyone but Calista. None of the others meant anything to me. I was vain, arrogant, pathetically insecure and incomprehensibly inconsiderate. And yet despite all that, her belief in my potential remained. It's partly what brought us here from New York to the islands, to *this* island."

Adele remained silent, allowing Decklan to gather his thoughts again before proceeding. His mind had retreated into the mist of memory—a journey he had struggled to avoid for a very long time.

"*Manitoba* was published just weeks before our marriage, and in the chaos of doing interviews and signings and other publicity obligations, we neglected to make time for a honeymoon. Actually, I'm not being entirely honest. I should say that *I* neglected to make time. The novel's success had been the culmination of what was then my life's dream. I embraced it like a starving man would a banquet laid out before him. I gorged myself on that success, became drunk off of it, and for a few precarious months, nearly lost myself entirely to it. If not for Calista, I most certainly would have. She was my figurative island, and then following our eventual honeymoon that brought us to this place, this became our literal island together. By then the novel was a bestseller, the money was beyond anything either of us could have thought possible, and our life here was…"

Decklan's voice trailed off and his eyes closed as he lifted his head slightly upward.

"What was your life here?" Adele asked.

Decklan's eyes remained closed. He grunted softly and then opened them, revealing he was on the verge of tears.

"It was perfect."

He paused again to wipe the corners of his eyes. He appeared unembarrassed over the show of emotion. There was no self-awareness, only sadness.

"Calista took to designing this house with such enthusiasm. We were free from the daily obligations and temptations of New York life. At that time there was no phone here. We had to take a small boat to Deer Harbor and use theirs so that I could check in with my publicist. Beyond that, our time was truly our own, and we felt like we had all the time in the world. And then when the dock was completed, we decided to purchase a larger boat to allow us to explore the entirety of the surrounding islands. We became frequent guests at Roche Harbor, Friday Harbor, Fisherman Bay, that wonderful resort in Rosario, and occasionally we journeyed to the Gulf Islands in Canada. We would fish and crab, explore beaches, and watch the whales, the birds, and the storms that made the waters churn and the skies darken like some great work of antediluvian art. I was as happy and content as any man could possibly be. She loved the boat, the water, the undeniable and mysterious beauty of this place, and we loved each other. We had become an island unto ourselves."

This time it took both of Decklan's hands to wipe the tears from his eyes.

"In the winter we would sit on a blanket in front of the fireplace there and happily empty a bottle of wine that we brought back from one of our boating excursions. Sometimes we would talk of things great and small, while other times we said very little and simply enjoyed the moment to ourselves.

"If I was particularly quiet, Calista would tease me that the world would shake its head if it were to learn that someone who so many perceived to be a man of great words was in fact such a mute. I would tell her that I would rather be a great man of few words, than simply another man of too many. She would fill this house with her laughter and declare me hopelessly convinced of my own intellectual superiority."

Decklan again looked to the outside world beyond the windows as his voice lowered to a barely audible whisper.

"I have missed her laughter for a very long time."

He cleared this throat as if trying to stem the bleeding of a particularly painful emotional wound.

"Calista was much loved among the people of the San Juans. Her natural light would shine upon anyone fortunate enough to know her. She was far more than merely the wife of the man everyone took to calling, *The Writer*. She had a unique knack, perhaps with no more than a smile or a kind word, to leave others feeling better having experienced her. If the locals took a vote to decide which of us could remain on the islands, I am certain I would have been the one forced from here every time."

"I've only seen pictures of course, but she was a beautiful woman," Adele said.

Decklan nodded and then stood up from his chair.

"Yes, she was. I would like to show you some of her *real* beauty, Ms. Plank. Would you mind if we took a bit of a walk?"

Adele looked up with an expression that spoke to her confused curiosity.

"You mean outside?"

Decklan held out his hand as he nodded.

"Yes, outside, as that is where I am able to feel her presence the most. I think it might help you to better understand my own story."

Adele felt Decklan's hand lightly grip her own. She delighted in the strength she felt as he easily pulled her up from the chair. His arm encircled her shoulders while his other hand pointed to the hallway that Adele knew connected to the kitchen. She was mildly disappointed in the almost fatherly way he gently led her along, devoid of even a hint of sexual attraction.

"Right this way," he said.

And what a kitchen it was. Decklan quickly took note of how it impressed his guest.

"Ah, yes, it's another extension of Calista. Inside the house, this was truly her place. She loved to cook, to take her coffee there at the breakfast nook with the view of the trees just outside. And look here at this sink."

Adele found herself unable to resist sharing in Decklan's enthusiasm for the large, stone-lined sink to the left of the high-end stainless stove.

"She discovered this on our way up to Martha's Vineyard the summer before we were married," Decklan said. "We later found out it was the sink from a colonial-era home in Boston. Can you imagine! It was one of those little roadside knick-knack shops, and they had this sink sitting outside, nearly overgrown with grass.

"Calista was instantly drawn to it and although it wasn't much to look at then, she demanded we buy it. We brought it back to New York, and then eventually it found its way here where one of the local artisans updated it to accommodate modern plumbing. She considered it the centerpiece for the entire kitchen. I would hear water running and Calista singing softly as she cleaned vegetables, watered a plant, or prepared a pot of coffee or some tea. She adored this sink."

Decklan turned the cold-water faucet on and let it run for a few seconds, smiling at the sound it made as the water hit the sink's highly polished stone. Then the smile faded as his hand lingered on the faucet handle for a moment longer.

"There is so much melancholy involved with remembering, isn't there? We have this ability to recall the things we once loved above all else but lack the ability to actually relive those moments. It's like the cruelest of mirages. We see it as it was but know it shall never be again. It makes one wish to never have remembered it at all."

Adele stood silently looking at the author's hand that remained resting atop the faucet handle. She found herself unable to adequately respond to an admission of such profound pain and so instead chose to simply wait for the dark cloud to pass and the light to once again return.

And so, it did. Decklan sighed, smiled, and then pointed to a single white door at the back corner of the kitchen.

"All right then," he said. "Outside we go."

4.

Adele delighted in the crisp, saltwater air that surrounded her outside Decklan's home. He slowly led her on the narrow, packed-earth paths that cut through the small island. She was fascinated by how quietly enthusiastic the author was when he stopped to show her a plant and explained why his wife had chosen it so many years earlier. Every location had a story, a memory, an integral piece of the woman with whom Decklan had so deeply loved.

He brought Adele down to the partially hidden cove she had noticed upon her arrival and spoke about the little runabout he kept on the cove's beach.

"It's a 1961, built nearby in Bellingham. I chose it because it was the very same year as the Chris Craft. Many times Calista would remain here on the island seeing to her plants and her gardens, while I took the runabout to set crab pots, pick up a bottle of wine from Deer Harbor, or, if I was feeling particularly adventurous, risk the larger waters off Point Doughty to the north and fish for salmon. She would scold me upon my return and beg that I please be more careful when out on the water alone."

Adele was smitten by the little watercraft and its graceful lines. She also noted how the grooves its bow cut into the beach's sand appeared relatively fresh and that the small outboard engine on the back looked new.

"You still take it out, don't you?"

Decklan ran his hand along the side of the runabout and then gave Adele a sheepish grin.

"Yes, quite often actually. My hermit-like existence is somewhat exaggerated by the locals. I am on the water two or three days a week, in fact. So much time has passed since Calista's death that some years ago I realized for those who come to the islands to merely vacation, I am as much a stranger to them as anyone else. I can visit the artists selling their wares at Roche Harbor, enjoy a fine meal in Friday Harbor, or even travel to the mainland in Anacortes in relative obscurity. I tasted notoriety, fame, and the admiration of many. For some time now I've also experienced obscurity. I prefer obscurity. It allows me to be myself and not have to consider what others would have me be."

Decklan's eyes suddenly widened, and he knelt down and picked up an inch-long piece of emerald-green sea glass. He held it in his hand, looking it over with eyes that gleamed like an excited boy who has just discovered something uniquely wonderful to the world. He then took Adele's hand, turned it over, and placed the glass in her palm.

"Here, something to remember me by."

Adele smiled, but a whisper of warning sounded from within her as she thanked him. She couldn't quite determine what it was that made her so uneasy at that moment. Then the discomfort passed, and Decklan made his way up the trail that led away from the beach. She placed the sea stone into her pocket as he called back to her.

"I saved the best for last. Let me show you Calista's special place."

Adele struggled to keep up as Decklan weaved between a pair of large tree trunks before finding yet another of the island's many trails. She noted how much easier it had become for him to speak of his wife in just the short time she had been there.

This is some kind of therapy for him, she thought. *Likely years of bottled-up pain and regret that he's finally letting out.*

"It's right over here!" Decklan shouted.

Adele looked up to see him standing between two weather-stained chairs that sat precariously close to a steep cliff that overlooked the waters below. She paused several feet from the chairs as she felt a familiar tightening in her stomach.

"Uh, I'm afraid of heights."

Decklan attempted a reassuring smile and waved Adele toward him.

"It's okay, I promise. Please, I'd like you to sit in one of the chairs. If you wish to understand more of who I was, and perhaps who I still am, *you need to do this.*"

Adele took a half step backward.

"I'm sorry. I can't. If I look down from there, I'll freak out. I'm not kidding."

The sound of water hitting the exposed rocks below drifted upward to Adele's ears, making her discomfort that much worse. Decklan extended his hand toward her.

"It's okay. I'll keep you safe."

Why is he being so insistent about this? Why does he want me so close to the cliff?

Adele began to wonder if Decklan Stone could in fact be a dangerous man capable of murder even as the normally more reasonable part of her nature refused the suggestion.

I'm acting like a frightened child. Stop being so pathetic.

"These chairs were custom made by a local artist," Decklan continued. "She's done several locations throughout the islands. They're handcrafted and then bolted right into the cliff rock. Calista would often sit out here in the late afternoon and watch the sun go down. Sometimes during a storm, we would both sit and look out at the lightning and feel the thunder as it shook the sky over our heads and listen as the waves crashed against the rocks below. During the busy summer months, we would admire all the different boats coming into Deer Harbor and wave at them as they passed our island. Come over here and you can look out and see it as she did."

Adele took another step back from what was feeling more and more like a decidedly dangerous brink from which she would never return.

"I said no."

Decklan's eyes widened and his mouth turned downward, marking his disappointment.

"I apologize. I frightened you. I had no intention of doing so."

Adele focused on keeping her breathing steady while trying to push away the panic that had nearly overtaken her.

Decklan took two cautious steps toward her.

"Ms. Plank, are you okay?"

Adele nodded.

"Yes, I'm fine. I'm sorry but my fear of heights can be overpowering sometimes. I feel a bit foolish."

Decklan held up both hands with the palms facing outward toward Adele.

"No, it was my fault. As soon as you indicated you weren't comfortable, I should have listened. It's been a very long time since I've had a guest here and I fear my enthusiasm overcame good manners and proper consideration."

He tilted his head to the side and his eyes narrowed slightly.

"Do you hear something?"

"Yes," Adele replied. "It sounds like a horn."

Decklan grunted as he moved past her and began to make his way back toward the house.

"I think you're right. It sounds as if it's coming from the dock."

Adele recalled Will Speaks telling her he would be back in three hours if he didn't hear from her sooner.

Both Decklan and Adele found Will standing next to his skiff, looking somewhat apprehensive. He straightened to his full height as Decklan began to make his way down the dock.

"Hello, Mr. Speaks."

Will's eyes refused to meet Decklan's gaze. Instead, he mumbled a reply while focusing his attention on Adele who stood a few paces behind the writer.

"Mr. Stone, I'm here like I promised Ms. Plank I would be. I'm just doing what I said I would."

Adele detected a bit of tension between the two men that bordered on outright animosity.

Decklan gave the skiff captain a thin smile.

"Thank you, Mr. Speaks. As you can see, my guest is both alive and well."

The animosity was no longer hinted. The author's tone relayed it loud and clear, leaving Adele to wonder about the lingering history between the author and Will Speaks.

"Are you ready, Ms. Plank? The tide will be changing soon and with the wind picking up it's likely to get a bit choppy. We best be on our way."

Decklan turned to face Adele. He cleared his throat, and then spoke in a lowered tone.

"If you would stay over as my guest tonight, I would be honored, Ms. Plank. I assure you my intentions are purely professional. The guest room is completely private. I can make us a meal, we can enjoy a bottle of wine, and I'll be more than happy to continue with the interview."

Will took a heavy step forward, an act which caused the dock to temporarily sway from side to side.

"I may not be available to pick you up tomorrow, Ms. Plank. We really should get going now."

Adele's silence let both men know she was considering Decklan's offer to stay overnight, which in turn caused Will's face reflect his near panic. Decklan folded his arms across his chest and smiled.

"It might save you some time and another trip out here if we just continue the interview into the evening. Of course, it's your decision."

A sudden gust of wind blew across the water, causing the Chris Craft to groan its discontent where it sat tied to the dock.

Will's voice cut through the din of the wind.

"See? We should be going *now*, Ms. Plank. A storm is coming. *Please*, I just want to do my job."

Why is he so afraid for me? Adele wondered. *Does he really think Decklan Stone is capable of doing me harm? Or is it something else I'm not seeing?*

"I'm quite certain Ms. Plank is capable of making up her own mind, Mr. Speaks."

Decklan Stone's tone issued the icy nature of his rebuke against Will's desire to see Adele taken from his private island. She watched, slightly stunned as Will clenched both of his fists tightly at his side. He appeared quite ready to use them. She knew there was some unknown conflict at play, something far greater than her immediate well-being. It was a mystery, and mysteries had long fascinated her.

"I'm going to accept Mr. Stone's offer and stay here tonight, Mr. Speaks. I'm sorry I wasn't able to let you know sooner, but the offer wasn't extended until just now."

Will's face contorted into a petulant snarl as he pointed at Decklan.

"I'll be telling my father about this. He won't like it one bit."

Adele's mouth fell open. Will suddenly appeared entirely absent the kindness and good nature she'd seen in him earlier. He looked like a man capable of almost anything, regardless of how dangerous that capability might prove.

Decklan stared back at the younger man without any sign of fear or intimidation.

"How *is* your father, Mr. Speaks? Has he recovered fully yet from the stroke?"

The corner of Will's mouth twitched as a hissing breath expelled from his lungs.

"He's doing just fine, *Mr. Stone.*

Decklan's face framed a thin, hard smile.

"That's good to hear. Now if you would like to keep your job with me, I suggest you get off my dock."

Will glanced over to where Adele stood motionless and silent.

"I'll be fine, Mr. Speaks," she said. "I'll call you in the morning and let you know when I'm ready to be taken back to Deer Harbor."

Will looked like he wanted to say more, but he simply nodded and stepped back onto his skiff. He started the outboard motor, steered the boat slowly away from the dock, and then gave both Decklan and Adele a lingering stare before pointing the small boat back toward the marina.

"Mr. Stone, are you going to tell me what that was all about?"

Decklan issued a long, weary sigh.

"*That* is a very long and troubling story."

"You've managed to do quite well for yourself sharing stories."

Decklan grinned.

"I suppose I have."

He looked up at the trees that swayed slowly in the breeze.

"It appears he was right."

Adele shivered as an especially cold blast of wind cut through her clothing.

"Right about what, Mr. Stone?"

Decklan gazed at the sky and its growing cacophony of wind and imminent rainfall.

"A storm is coming."

5.

Through the gaps in the bedroom blinds Adele watched the faint glow of orange-hued cigarette light outside for nearly twenty minutes. Her alcohol-drenched mind clumsily replayed the dinner and wine she had earlier shared with Decklan.

He had been both a gracious and talented host. His wine selection perfectly matched a meal of pan-roasted duck breast with goat cheese and cherries and a side of fresh greens delivered from the Orcas Island market.

By the time they opened the second bottle of wine, Decklan's initial relicence was further diminished, and he began to share a stream of memories, thoughts, and loosely linked recollections with his guest. Following his fifth glass of wine, he hinted again at the events surrounding his wife's death.

"Only if you're comfortable," Adele said. "Otherwise, we can wait and discuss it another time."

Decklan took a sip of wine and issued a very brief, almost imperceptible wince followed by a quick shake of his head.

"No, we can talk about it, what little there is to talk about."

His voice withered into silence. Adele sat across the small dining table with her hands folded in front of her. When Decklan finally spoke, she realized how tense her body had become, and then glanced down to make certain the recorder was on.

"We were up early that day because we intended to make Roche Harbor before the tide change. Docking is a lot easier during slack tide, so we wanted to arrive by late morning. Everything takes a little longer on a boat. You check the bilge, the fluid levels, let the engines warm up, untie, and finally you're on your way. The journey was fantastic. Calm water, a surprisingly warm morning breeze, and we even saw a small pod of whales as we neared Spieden Channel right before the entrance to Roche Harbor."

Decklan emptied half the wine from his glass and then his chin fell toward his chest as if retelling the events made him too weak to lift his head.

"Calista was beautiful, as always. She adored Roche and the people there loved her just as much. It reminded her of Sag Harbor and the Hamptons, places she went with her family to as a child. We were both in good spirits, happy, rested, and looking forward to a day in Roche. I captained the Chris Craft through the water at a comfortable eight knots. Soon we were tied up at the guest dock and greeted by our friend, Tilda, who owns the Roche Harbor Hotel."

"This Tilda, does she still own it?"

Decklan nodded.

"Yes, I believe so, though I haven't spoken to her for many years. She was a beautiful woman back then. Red-haired, tall, athletic, a transplant from the East Coast the same as Calista and me. Her parents had purchased the hotel years earlier and she, being their only child, inherited it. Initially, her parents still owned it, but by then they spent a lot of time in New York, so Tilda had become the face of the business. It was a pleasant enough face. It suited her."

"And Tilda and your wife were friends?"

Again, Decklan nodded.

"Yes, good friends. Tilda was just a few years older, so they shared much in common."

Adele noted how Decklan paused, making her mind work double time trying to read between the lines.

"We had brunch at the café overlooking the marina, a few laughs, and then Calista went to use the hotel phone to call a taxi to take her to Friday Harbor on the other side of the island. There was a bookstore there, and she had ordered a copy of something she wanted to read, I believe it might have been Updike's, *Couples.* She didn't elaborate much on why she was going to the bookstore. I personally knew Updike enough to say I didn't care for him, and Calista was somewhat sensitive toward my opinion on the matter."

"And what did you do while she was in Friday Harbor?"

Decklan emptied the second bottle of wine into his glass and took another drink.

"Yes, an appropriate question, isn't it? I stayed back at the boat to do various chores. There is always something that needs to be done on a boat. Those who've haven't owned one could never possibly understand. I didn't mind. I rather enjoy it. More often than not, I would end up talking with another boater on the dock, exchanging water stories and such. Truth be told, it's a wonderful existence, a day on the dock in a place like Roche Harbor. I highly recommend it."

Adele pretended to take a drink from her nearly full glass, but it was a deceptive gesture. Her head was already buzzing, and she didn't want her mind further degraded by the effects of yet more alcohol. She wanted to keep her clarity intact as Decklan continued to tell the story of the day his wife died.

"And then what happened? Did Calista return to the boat?"

Decklan winced again as a soft grunt passed between his pursed lips.

"Yes, right on time with book in hand. I wasn't on the boat though."

"Where were you?"

Decklan took another drink.

"I was up at the hotel."

Adele's brows arched.

"With Tilda?"

Decklan shot her a disapproving glance. He didn't care for what the question insinuated, even though he understood her reason for asking.

"I was at the hotel washing a cut on my hand. I had been replacing an exhaust hose, and one of the clamps had broken, leaving a sharpened edge that caused a sizable gash. There wasn't a medical kit on the boat so I went to see Tilda, thinking she might have one I could use."

"And that's when your wife found you with Tilda in the hotel?"

Decklan made no attempt to hide the annoyance in his voice.

"Yes, Tilda was bandaging my hand. That is *all* she was doing."

Outside the home, a small tree branch was being pushed up against the side of the house by the wind.

"Was your wife unhappy to see you alone with her?"

Decklan swirled the remaining wine in his glass as his eyes moved slowly upward toward Adele.

"No, not just yet. She wasn't angry until later. In fact, we had dinner with Tilda and then hurried to get to the boat so we could make the trip back home before nightfall. We started to argue as soon as Tilda was no longer around. Calista drank quite a bit during dinner, and I had drunk too much as well. Neither of us was in any condition to be on the water, but there we were in near darkness, making our way back here to the island. I was at the helm above while she stayed in the aft cabin down below. Every few minutes she would come up to accuse me of having another affair, and I would take that as my cue to have another drink from a bottle of scotch I had opened just before leaving Roche Harbor."

Decklan put his wine glass down and then pushed it away with a look of disgust.

"I was drunk. We both were, but unlike Calista, it was *my* responsibility to get us home safely. I failed to do so."

Adele didn't realize she had been holding her breath until she took a much-needed gulp of air. The media coverage of Calista Stone's death had never mentioned her husband being under the influence of alcohol when she reportedly fell off the Chris Craft at night. She was now hearing Decklan Stone's true confession.

"At the halfway point back, Calista stopped coming up to the bridge to yell at me," Decklan continued. "I assumed she had fallen asleep. Traveling on the boat often made her sleepy. So, I continued moving toward Orcas Island. I remember passing the southern tip of Jones Island and then entering Deer Harbor. The weather was fine; there was even a bit of moonlight to help illuminate the way home."

Adele cleared her throat and leaned forward in the chair across the kitchen table from where Decklan sat.

"And did you keep drinking during that time?"

Decklan looked away, wanting to avoid his shame reflected back at him in Adele's eyes.

"Yes," he whispered.

Then his nostrils flared and his jaw clenched as he growled the same word.

"*Yes*, I...kept...drinking. So much so, I can barely recall tying up to the dock. I knocked on the side of the boat, called out for Calista to come out, and then, in a fit of stupid anger, thought I was leaving her there. I went up to the house without her. I left my wife alone that night without making certain she was okay. Why? To this day I can't explain it."

"But she had likely already fallen off the boat by then."

Decklan stared up at the ceiling and shook his head.

"True, but if I had known she wasn't on the boat, there may still have been time to save her. Calista wasn't a terribly strong swimmer, but strong enough to at least give herself a chance. She needed someone to come find her, someone to save her. It should have been me. My behavior, my horrible, irresponsible behavior left her to die, struggling in those midnight waters until she could struggle no more."

He rose from the table, lifted his arms, and extended them outward from both sides of his body.

"You see, Ms. Plank, the rumors are true. I *am* a murderer. I killed my wife."

Adele watched silently as Decklan lowered his arms and swayed from side to side on unsteady legs as he again appeared on the verge of tears.

"Most people have the privilege of waking up *from* a nightmare. The next morning, I woke up *to* one. Calista's side of the bed remained empty. I was sober enough by then to realize how irresponsible I had been. I made my way back to the boat and then found it empty as well. I called out for her, looked throughout the house and all over the island. She was gone. I panicked, not wanting to think the worst, but knowing it to be a possible explanation for her absence.

"I called the police, explained to them our return from Roche Harbor and that she might have gone missing at some point during that time. The dispatcher suggested that perhaps Calista had simply called over to Deer Harbor for a ride to the main island. I was embarrassed to have not thought of that possibility. In fact, I then believed that had to have been what happened. The county sheriff called me back to say no such call by Calista had been made, and my worst fears returned. The sheriff took over from there and within the hour, initiated a search party of several boats that covered the entirety of the waters between here and Roche Harbor."

"And was that Sheriff Speaks, Will's father? The one you questioned Will about having a stroke?"

Decklan grunted.

"Yeah."

"You don't like him?"

Decklan folded his arms across his chest and looked away, letting Adele know he was thinking of ending the interview.

I can't let that happen, she told herself.

"Did he arrest you?"

Decklan's eyes flashed anger.

"*No*, that was never a possibility. Sheriff Speaks interviewed me later that day and then had me come to Friday Harbor for a follow-up interview the following day. By then Calista had been designated as missing and likely dead. The sheriff said they found one of her shoes floating in the water about a mile from Deer Harbor. She was gone. I kept looking for her though. The authorities, the sheriff, they just stopped. He insisted she couldn't have survived, not for that long. The sheriff was the one who finally convinced me of the worst, and I suppose I've never really forgiven him for being the bearer of that terrible news."

"So, case closed, just like that?"

Decklan nodded and his shoulders slumped, looking every inch the broken man.

"Yeah, just like that. The official report indicated it to be death by accidental drowning."

Adele's brow furrowed. She sensed something was being left out. Decklan saw the gesture and then sat back down in his chair.

"You have good instincts for knowing when you're not being told the whole story."

Adele folded her hands in front of her, looking and sounding far more fearless than she in fact felt.

"Why don't you go ahead and tell me the *whole* story, Mr. Stone?"

Decklan repeatedly tapped the top of the table while he considered the request. He stared into Adele's eyes for several seconds, gave her a pained smile, and then abruptly stood back up.

"Albert Camus said that one needs more courage to live than to die. I think I've lived just long enough to finally and fully understand that sentiment. I am not a man of courage, Ms. Plank. It's been a long day and I've grown very, very tired. The thirtieth anniversary of *Manitoba,* what brought you here, is for me more burden than remembrance; it requires reliving things I have spent much of my life trying to forget. There comes a point when one simply wants to rest, you know? To silence the voices of discontent, loss, and guilt that grow louder and more abusive with each unfortunate day."

Decklan turned and made his way upstairs, while his parting words continued to echo in Adele's mind as she watched the burning cigarette outside her window.

He wants to die. I'm to be his final interview and then he's going to kill himself. When he gave me the beach glass, he said it would be something to remember him by.

The thought horrified Adele, but just below the surface of that horror was fascination, which in turn disgusted her.

I can't believe I'm thinking how much his death would help my career. Since when did I become such a cold bitch who would put someone's well-being beneath my own motivation for success?

Decklan was clearly a man in terrible pain. He needed help. And yet, Adele knew there was much to the story of his wife's death that still remained untold.

The cigarette burned bright. Decklan was taking a particularly strong drag as a sudden gust of wind pushed its way through the island trees.

Adele turned away from the guest room window after hearing the sound of a door opening down the hallway.

The door to Decklan's room," she thought.

The hairs on the back of her neck stood up as she slowly backed away from the window.

If Decklan is in the house, then who the hell is that smoking a cigarette outside?

Someone else was on the island with them.

6.

By the time Adele returned to the window, the cigarette light had vanished. She scampered back to the guest room door and peered down the long, wood-floored hallway. It remained empty and no other sounds interrupted the interior silence.

She shut the door as quietly as possible and turned the handle to the lock position, grateful for the comforting click.

Adele spent the remainder of the night and early morning tossing and turning. She considered waking Decklan and telling him about what she saw outside but decided it would be unwise to have him wandering the island inebriated and while still so emotionally raw.

As soon as daylight pushed back the shadows of night, Adele rose up from the bed and peered out the second-story window again. She found the area below absent of anything but yellowed island grass, framed by a backdrop of tall trees.

The storm from the night before had passed, replaced by the bright and considerably more cheerful presence of the San Juan Island sun.

Adele turned at the sound of a light knock from the other side of the bedroom door.

"Yes?"

"Ms. Plank, I'll be making some coffee and toast. Would you like some?"

"Yes, thank you."

Decklan sounded no worse for wear, despite the previous night's drinking.

Unlike me who feels more than ready to go back to bed.

After a quick shower and change of clothes, Adele was once again seated at the kitchen table.

"I hope you slept okay. If you're anything like me, getting a good night's sleep outside of your own bed can be something of a chore."

Adele sipped from the strong cup of coffee Decklan had made and then nibbled the corner off a piece of whole-wheat toast. He smelled of soap and was dressed casually in faded blue jeans and a black Rolling Stones t-shirt from the 1970s. Adele was pleasantly surprised to see how sinewy and well-developed his arms were.

"Actually, I thought I saw someone standing outside the house smoking last night right below my window."

Decklan's hand, which held a piece of toast, paused halfway between plate and mouth.

"Really? What did they look like?"

Adele shrugged.

"It was too dark to tell. I'm pretty sure it was a man, but I couldn't see his face. I thought it was you at first. And then I thought I might have just been seeing something that wasn't really there. You really weren't outside smoking last night?"

Decklan's brow furrowed as he contemplated what Adele told him.

"I've been trying to quit for some time. I *did* have one cigarette before bed, but I wasn't outside. Are you certain you saw someone?"

Adele nodded.

"I'm almost positive there was a man standing beneath the trees next to the house."

Decklan frowned.

"Well, that's rather troubling. We'll have to take a quick look before you head out today. Would you be able to show me exactly where you think you saw him standing?"

Adele nodded again.

"Sure, that should be easy enough."

The two sat in silence and finished their coffee and toast and then Adele cleared her throat, signaling she had another question.

"Why haven't you just left the island? From what you said last night, it seems clear there are a lot of painful memories for you here. Why not just pack up and go somewhere else?"

Decklan leaned back in the cream-colored, farmhouse-styled wood chair and closed his eyes. Only after those eyes opened did he give his reply.

"I did try that once, about ten years ago. I packed a suitcase and took the runabout all the way over to Anacortes in a bad storm. In fact, I just about swamped her on the way there after taking quite a bit of water over the bow. I think part of me wanted to go down somewhere too far away to swim to shore. I made it though. I remember it well. I was standing on the dock in Anacortes looking out at the storm and had this overwhelming sense I was leaving Calista behind, that I was abandoning her. My intention was to fly back to New York and try to start over there. My publisher, my publicist, my accountant, they were all for it. But the more I stood on that dock getting soaked by rain, the more I knew that leaving here wasn't an option. It would *never* be an option for me. I'll die here, just like Calista."

Adele leaned forward.

"Do you *want* to die, Decklan? Is that what this is about—the interview? Allowing me to come here? Is it some kind of last word before you finish yourself off? Because if it is, *I want no part of it*."

Decklan appeared ready to say something but instead tipped his head toward the door to the area behind the house.

"How about we go take a look outside?"

Adele wasn't satisfied. He was avoiding her question, but she didn't want to push a subject Decklan clearly didn't wish to speak about.

"Okay."

She followed Decklan outside and then took him to the spot below her window. He squatted down, ran his hand along the ground and then snatched something from between the trampled blades of grass.

"It appears you saw what you saw, Ms. Plank."

He held up a faded orange cigarette butt.

"Any idea who it was?" Adele asked.

Even as Decklan shook his head, Adele felt he was again hiding something from her.

"No, but it's certainly unusual."

Decklan glanced at his Rolex.

"How about I take you over to Deer Harbor myself? There's no need to have Mr. Speaks make his way back here."

It took no more than thirty minutes for Adele to gather her belongings and follow Decklan to the little beach where the runabout sat waiting. He handed her an inflatable life preserver.

"Please put this on."

Adele did as she was told and carefully boarded the boat where she took her place on a bench at the back by the engine. Decklan untied the rope that held the boat to a tree and pushed against the bow until half the runabout was in the water. He climbed in from the side and sat down in the small vinyl chair in front of the helm. Adele watched as he grasped the single lever control that was screwed into the upper right side of the fiberglass hull's interior. Decklan pushed a button on the lever and the small outboard motor lowered into the water.

Once the outboard's prop was fully submerged, he started the motor. Adele was surprised at how quiet it was. It was almost silent, especially compared to Will's skiff. Decklan turned around to make certain she was seated. Then he bumped the outboard into reverse and back to neutral. He repeated this for a second time, and then a third. Each time he did so, the runabout backed farther into the water until finally there was enough distance from the beach to turn the boat and point it toward the Deer Harbor marina.

Decklan turned around to face Adele.

"Should we take the more scenic route?"

Adele smiled.

"You're the captain."

Adele marveled at Decklan's sudden transformation. The melancholy shadow had vanished from his eyes, replaced by a calm satisfaction that, Adele suspected, came from being on the water. He appeared completely at home behind the wheel while he steered the boat to the right and then pushed the control lever forward, accelerating until the drone of the engine mingled with the whoosh of chilly morning wind that caused Adele's eyes to water and her nose to run.

The runabout's bow lifted upward a few feet and then lowered with a pronounced slap against the water. The movement repeated again and again as Decklan steered the craft toward the shoreline on the opposite side of the bay. Adele saw a bald eagle flying no more than forty feet above her head before it moved toward a wall of trees that sprung up just above the shore.

Decklan's grin expanded into a broad smile as he pointed at a cluster of dark rocks that broke the surface of the water some fifty yards from where the small boat was passing by.

"Check them out!" he exclaimed. "The basset hounds of the sea!"

Three large seals were laid out upon the rocks like wet, glistening sausages, enjoying the emerging warmth of the morning sun.

All three of the sea mammals lifted their heads in unison to watch the boat speed by. Adele found herself unable to resist waving at them like a child overcome with the joy of seeing something wholly unexpected.

Decklan chuckled as he watched Adele wave at the seals and then he quickly turned away as he was hit with a particularly powerful sense of déjà vu. Long ago his wife Calista would react with a very similar kind of joy in response to the beauty of the islands.

Even though she couldn't see his face, Adele felt the change in Decklan's mood and just as quickly guessed the reason why.

He's remembering being out here with his wife.

The runabout made a circular half-turn and began to head toward Deer Harbor at a reduced speed with Decklan silently staring through the boat's small plastic windscreen. Within five minutes he was pulling up slowly alongside the unloading area at the marina's guest dock which he then tied up to.

"Safely arrived, Ms. Plank."

Decklan hopped onto the dock, and then extended his hand to help Adele off the boat.

"When can I come back and continue the interview?" she asked.

He looked up at a pair of seagulls passing overhead and shrugged.

"Oh, I'll be in touch."

"Can I get your cell number?"

Decklan shook his head.

"Don't have one. I find that smartphones make for stupid people. Present company excluded, of course."

Adele almost laughed.

"Of course."

"Do you need help getting a taxi to the ferry?"

Deer Harbor was a few miles drive from the Orcas Island ferry terminal.

"No," Adele replied. "I'll call for one."

She extended her hand toward Decklan. Instead of shaking hands he spread his arms and wrapped them around Adele in a light hug. She caught a whiff of his cologne, felt the warmth of his body, and secretly wished he found her more attractive.

"I appreciate your patience with me, Ms. Plank. I *will* be in touch. I promise."

When Decklan pulled away, Adele pointed at his chest.

"I am going to hold you to that, Mr. Decklan Stone."

She began to make her way up the ramp with her backpack hanging off her shoulders. Halfway up she turned around and saw Decklan watching her departure. He smiled and gave her a thumbs-up. Adele mimicked the gesture before continuing toward the road. She made certain her cell phone had a signal and then made a quick call to the taxi service that had brought her to Deer Harbor the previous day, recalling that the driver's name as Joe.

Joe answered on the first ring and said he would be there in twenty minutes.

"Ms. Plank, is that you?"

Adele turned around toward the marina below and saw Will Speaks staring back at her.

"Oh, hello Mr. Speaks. Yes, it's me. Uh, Mr. Stone brought me back himself."

Will squinted up at her looking less than pleased by her comment.

"Really? Wow, I don't think I've ever heard of him doing that before. That's kind of weird. Hey, you mind if I introduce you to my father? He's right down there in the slip on the other side of the store."

Adele realized she was going to meet the San Juan County sheriff who led the investigation into Calista Stone's death. She also recalled that the retired sheriff had recently suffered a stroke.

"Sure, I'll meet him if you think he won't mind."

Will motioned for Adele to follow and walked toward the Deer Harbor General Store, a small, square, wood-framed structure that boasted of having the best ice cream on the island.

"Oh, he won't mind. In fact, he already said he should see you when he found out you were talking to the writer."

Adele had to quicken her pace to keep up with Will's strides. He made a sharp turn and then galloped down a steep, steel-grate ramp that led to another set of floating boat slips.

"Hey, Dad, I have that pretty little reporter with me."

Adele looked down the dock and saw an older, thinner version of Will Speaks stepping off a badly dented fishing boat. A cigarette hung from the corner of his downturned mouth and two dark eyes stared at her from beneath the brim of a sweat-stained baseball cap. Several days' growth of silver whiskers lined his haggard face, and Adele noted that his right leg had a slight limp.

"You're the reporter, huh?"

The former sheriff's voice was a low, sandpaper-like rasp. A nicotine cloud halo hung over his head, and he smelled very much like a wet ashtray mixed with sweat and sickness.

"I'm from the university in Bellingham. My name is Adele Plank."

"I'm Martin but you can just call me Sheriff. That's what everyone still knows me by. I suppose after thirty-six years of wearing the badge I deserve that bit of respect, right?"

Adele found herself nodding and taking a step back at the same time.

"Nice to meet you, Sheriff."

Martin grunted and then straightened his bent back as best he could while keeping his dark eyes boring into Adele's.

"What did you and the writer talk about?"

Adele looked down at her feet, feeling like a young child caught doing something wrong.

"It was an interview, just the first one."

Martin stepped toward Adele and glared at her with even greater intensity.

"The *first* one? You mean you intend to go back to that island again? Now why would a nice young woman like you want to do something so foolish as that?"

Adele told herself not to take another step back. She didn't want to appear any weaker.

"I'm sorry?"

Martin glanced at his son and shook his head.

"No, we can't have any more of that, young lady. You got your one interview. Hell, *you spent the night with the man*! I think that's gonna have to be it. Is that understood?"

"You leave her alone, Martin Speaks! Stop being a grumpy old cuss!"

Adele turned to see an elderly woman walking toward them.

"Don't you give me the stink-eye, Sheriff! I can hear you playing tough guy all the way from my store. Now get on and leave this girl alone. She's just doing a job and it's no business of yours."

Martin rolled his eyes and opened his mouth to protest but was quickly cut off by the feisty store owner.

"I don't want to hear it, Martin! Get back on your boat there and pretend to work on it like you always do, even though we all know you're just wasting time. That bucket hasn't been out of its slip in ages."

The woman appeared to be well into her seventies. She had thin, wispy-grey hair that was cut short, bright blue-green eyes, and a firm, thin-lipped mouth. She was just over five feet, narrow-hipped, and someone who clearly had little fear of anything or anyone.

"Hello, young lady, my name is Bella Morris. I own that little shack up there and have since me and my husband, God rest his soul, bought it about, oh, forty-odd years ago when it was hardly more than a lean-to that the fishermen used to buy their supplies from. You want some ice cream? We have the best on the island and that's not bragging—it's a fact."

Adele smiled, immediately charmed by the new arrival.

"That sounds great. My name is Adele. My taxi will be here soon, though."

The sheriff cleared his throat.

"I'm not done making my point, Bella."

Bella stepped between Adele and Martin and then placed a hand on each of her thin hips.

"Oh yes you *are*, Sheriff. There will be no more of you telling, uh, telling…"

Adele realized the older woman had already forgotten her name.

"Adele."

Bella nodded her head and then glowered at the retired sheriff.

"Adele! That's right. You won't be telling Adele here what her business is because it's not for you to decide. And stop blowing that god-awful cigarette smoke in my face. You would think after the stroke you would have given those coffin nails up. Now go."

Martin threw his hands up while muttering something inaudible under his breath. He shuffled back toward his boat, and then turned around and pointed at Adele.

"You make any plans to be back on that island talking to the writer you see me first, understood? You got my boy's number. You let Will know and he'll let me know. And a word of advice you'd do well to follow—don't go pissing me off. There are plenty of people around here who are smart enough to follow that advice, and I expect you're just smart enough to do the same."

Bella gave a disgusted sigh.

"Shame on you, Martin. My patience with you has run out."

"Actually, Sheriff Speaks," Adele said, "I would like to sit down and interview you as well. I figure you could fill in a lot of the details regarding the investigation into, Mrs. Stone's death. If we could schedule—"

Martin took two shuffle-strides toward where Adele and Bella stood, his eyes lit by some terrible agitation.

"Why would you bring *that* up? Why in the hell would you think I'd want to talk about such a thing? It's time for you to leave young lady—NOW."

Bella pushed Adele forward and whispered a warning.

"He's about ready to blow. He might just kill you or himself, so I suggest you do as he says and get moving."

"Good-bye, Ms. Plank!" Will Speaks shouted.

Adele waved good-bye to him while Martin poked a finger into Will's side with enough force to cause his middle-aged son to flinch.

"Don't you even think about it!"

Think about it? Adele wondered. *What's that supposed to mean?*

She wasn't given time to find out. Bella continued pushing her up the ramp toward the small store.

"He's a grumpy old fool, but normally not that aggressive. I wonder what it is about you that bothers him so much?"

Adele shrugged and watched Bella disappear behind the old, nicked and gouged wood counter that separated the store's main area from a tiny kitchen space in the back. The entirety of the store area consisted of three handmade wood shelves with the bare essentials: bread, canned goods, and a surprisingly large selection of wine. When Bella remerged, she was holding an ice cream cone with a single scoop of vanilla.

"It's never too early in the day for ice cream."

Adele thanked her and peered through the store's open entrance toward the road to confirm her taxi hadn't yet arrived. Then she turned her full attention to the elderly store owner.

"Do you know Decklan Stone?"

Bella nodded.

"The writer? Oh, yes, he's been coming here off and on for years, usually when there's not many others around. I knew him and his wife when they first arrived to the islands. Such a tragic thing. She was so beautiful and liked by everyone."

Adele tilted her head toward the direction of Martin Speaks.

"Even that sheriff character?"

Bella glanced outside to make sure nobody was close enough to overhear the conversation.

"Old Martin wasn't always old, you know. He was a good-looking fella, in fact. There was a time when he filled out a uniform rather nicely. He loved wearing that badge and carrying a gun and he kept this place safe for a long time, especially during the summer season when we need it the most. As for his views of Mrs. Stone, I seem to recall him liking her well enough. She always showed Will great kindness. Will can hide it better these days, but he was born simple and used to have a terrible stutter. When he was younger, he was often teased by the other children. Even in his late teens he was very awkward and uncertain and acted much younger than his years. Mrs. Stone made certain to always give Will that big, warm smile of hers with lots of positive reinforcement and you could see the change in Will, how he was more confident around her, almost like a normal young man would be. I'm certain the sheriff took note of that and appreciated it. It likely wasn't easy for him raising that boy on his own."

"What happened to Will's mother?"

Bella folded her arms across her chest and frowned.

"Oh, that happened shortly before I arrived here with my husband. My understanding is that she died during childbirth and poor Will almost died too. Had the umbilical cord around his neck and it about choked the life out of him, poor thing.

"So there was Martin and this little boy living all alone out in the middle of the island on the big old farm Martin inherited from his parents when they passed. He's sold some of it off over the years, but it still has to be a good forty acres at least. His family was one of the very first to settle the island."

Adele was disappointed to see the taxi arrive. Bella was proving to be a wealth of information.

"Damn, my taxi is here. Bella, thank you so much for the ice cream and the conversation. Would it be possible for us to continue talking when I come back?"

Bella's deeply lined face lit up at the compliment.

"I would like that very much! I'll be here waiting, God willing."

Adele was almost to the taxi when she turned around and saw Will Speaks standing no more than twenty feet behind her. He appeared nervous, his eyes glancing down at his feet.

"I'm sorry about my dad, Ms. Plank. He doesn't mean any real harm. He just wants what's best. He protects people and keeps them safe."

Adele didn't understand why she suddenly felt threatened, but the feeling persisted.

"That's okay, Will. And thank you again for taking me to the island yesterday."

Adele moved to open the taxi door when Will's voice stopped her.

"When will I see you again, Ms. Plank? You a-a-a-*are* coming back, right?"

Adele gave a brief, troubled nod.

This is getting weird. And there's the stutter Bella told me about that Will had when he was younger.

"Yes, I think so."

Will took two steps toward Adele and then stopped. He appeared to be fighting some enemy within himself as he slowly rubbed his large hands over the sides of his blue jeans.

"My dad said to let me know. You remember that, right? You don't want to piss him off. That's what he said."

Adele continued looking at Will while reaching behind to open the taxi door. Will's friendly, red-cheeked face was transformed. It was now the visage of a man on the verge of doing terrible violence. He lowered his head, narrowed his eyes, and balled his hands into tight, trembling fists.

"Is everything okay? We need to get going if you're going to catch the next ferry," said Joe, the taxi driver.

Adele let out a deep breath. She hadn't realized she'd been holding it in. Will blinked several times as if waking from a dream and then gave a wide smile to the taxi driver.

"Hey, Joe, how are you doing?"

Joe gave Will a quick, dismissive nod and then looked at Adele.

"You ready to go?"

Adele nodded and shut the door behind her, grateful to be inside the taxi. As the car pulled away from the marina, she looked back through the rear window and saw Will Speaks standing in the middle of the road watching her departure.

He wasn't smiling.

7.

The following day.

Shortly after she arrived as an undergraduate student at Bellingham University, Adele had chosen the basement-level media archives section of the college's expansive, red-bricked library as her primary place of study. It wasn't just the quiet solitude of the four thousand square foot space that appealed to her, but the smell of the newspapers, magazines, and various other publications that were housed within massive and carefully organized rolling shelves by date and title. It was the aged paper scent of once-living and breathing moments that were, through the cruelty that is the passage of time, demoted to mere remnants of history that she found so fascinating to look over and study.

Her favorite desk was located at the very back wall of the basement which afforded her a small window through which she could look up and see the feet of people passing by from outside. She would sometimes watch the different shoes flash across the window and wonder what kind of lives those shoes were a part of, where they had travelled, and what future paths yet awaited them.

On this night, though, Adele wasn't focused on footwear. Instead, she was looking up at a boxed collection of a Parisian arts and fashion magazine that had been discontinued for more than twenty years. She had taken two years of French in high school, so was able to slowly and clumsily follow the text.

It wasn't the words but rather the pictures within a feature on a then-emerging American author Adele was most interested in. The article had been written twenty-eight years earlier, almost two years after the publication of Decklan Stone's, *Manitoba*.

The magazine's feature on Decklan was accompanied by several large black and white photographs. Adele stared down at a young and vibrant Decklan dressed in cargo shorts and a light sweater smiling back at the camera with the idyllic, time-capsule quality of the Roche Harbor resort as a backdrop. The next photo had Decklan and Calista holding hands as they walked toward the Roche Harbor Hotel. And a third picture depicted the couple standing on the bow of the very same Chris Craft Adele had so recently seen on her trip to the writer's private island in Deer Harbor. Decklan's eyes appeared to be scanning the world laid out before him while Calista's eyes were fixed on her husband.

They both look so impossibly beautiful and happy.

Even as Adele formed that thought, she was simultaneously reminded that Calista Stone would be dead within a year of when that photograph was taken.

She reached across her small desk and pulled an archived copy of the Island Gazette that featured the story of Calista Stone's tragic demise. Adele looked up as the florescent light that hung from the ceiling over her head buzzed, popped, and threatened to go out before resuming its faint-droning illumination.

Adele had read the very same article prior to her initial interview with Decklan Stone, but now, after having actually met him, she wished to revisit it:

Wife Of Renowned Author Feared Dead

Local authorities called off a twelve-hour search for twenty-seven-year-old Calista Stone, wife of best-selling author, Decklan Stone. Mr. and Mrs. Stone were returning from a day trip to Roche Harbor from their island retreat located a short distance away in Deer Harbor on Orcas Island. It is believed she fell from the boat and then drowned.

Stone, a New York native, had become a common sight among island locals after recently moving to the area with her famous novelist husband. She was noted for her interest in helping local charities and forging new friendships with many of the area business owners.

San Juan Island County Sheriff Martin Speaks issued an official update late yesterday indicating there was no evidence of foul play. The death had been ruled an accident, thus ending the investigation.

Mr. Stone's publicist sent out the following statement to both local and national media regarding the incident:

Decklan Stone has requested privacy following his beloved Calista's tragic passing this past week. Per his wife's wishes, there will be no service.

Adele looked at the bottom of the page and saw a photograph of a much younger looking Martin Speaks holding up a single shoe with the following caption below the picture:

Sheriff Speaks holding the only thing found following the search for Calista Stone, a shoe that Mr. Stone later identified as belonging to his wife.

The sound of approaching footsteps echoed off the hard, linoleum floor of the hallway that led to the media archives room. Adele waited to see if anyone would appear. Soon, she heard the soft ding of the elevator located down the hall beyond the room's entrance.

She then heard the sound of something scraping the sidewalk surface above her and looked up through the window to see a scuffed black boot putting out a cigarette. It was a familiar sight as the area was a common place for smokers. Adele realized how late it was as she noted the darkness outside. As so often happened in the archives room, she had lost herself in research, and in doing so, let the time get away from her.

It was well past the library's normal operating hours. For Adele it was not an uncommon occurrence to have to make her way outside after both students and staff had already left the library for the night. She carefully placed the magazine and newspaper into her backpack and then stood up from the desk just as the light once again began to flicker on and off.

Adele would be the first to admit that no matter how many times she was alone in the library, it was no less creepy. She looked up at the window; there were no longer any people passing by outside. The university campus was settling in for the night.

More footsteps could be heard echoing against the walls in the hallway outside of the archive room. Adele listened while sitting very still.

Someone is coming down the stairs.

Whoever it was they were moving slowly, as if uncertain where they were going. Without knowing why, Adele felt a tightening in her throat and the sudden urge to hide.

She moved as quietly as possible between the four-foot-wide space that separated the multiple rolling shelves and made her way toward the very back of the archives room. There she crouched behind multiple stacks of *LIFE* magazine periodicals and waited.

Adele could hear the footsteps more clearly. Their pace remained slow and deliberate, and appeared to turn left down the hallway before abruptly moving back toward, and then finally into, the archive room. Whoever it was paused just underneath the doorway entrance.

They're looking to see if anyone is in here. Maybe it's just a janitor or security, or—

The footsteps resumed. They were heavy enough that Adele felt certain it was a man—a man who was now inside the archive room no more than forty feet from where she hid.

I need to get a look at who it is.

Adele slowly rose from her crouch and attempted to move her head just enough to see down the rows of shelves.

The florescent light above the desk proceeded to snap and flutter, and then it abruptly went out with a final pop, making it impossible for Adele to see who might be walking toward her.

The footsteps continued.

Adele again crouched low and tried to be as still as possible as she realized the man was no more than four rows away from her hiding spot. He was, in fact, close enough that she could smell the cigarette smoke on him.

She proceeded to crawl on all fours to the end of the bookshelf and then curled into a ball against the corner of the shelf and wall, praying the darkness would keep her from being seen.

Adele looked up as the man's approach suddenly halted. A form, partially hidden by shadow, stood at the end of the row and seemed to be staring directly at her. He wore a dark hoodie pulled over his head, making it impossible to see the face residing within. Adele opened her mouth and prepared to scream as loud as she could.

The sound of the elevator opening in the hallway outside the room caused her to pause and the man to suddenly turn and make his way toward the exit.

"Excuse me, sir, the library is closed. You're not supposed to—"

Just as Adele stood up, she heard a body striking against something hard and an older male voice crying out at someone.

"Hey! Get your ass back here!"

Adele ran down the space between the shelves toward the archive room entrance and saw a man struggling to get back onto his feet. She leaned down to help him, but when he looked up at her he pushed her hand away.

"And what the hell are *you* doing down here? Up to no good, I suppose?"

The man, who was in his late sixties, winced as he he stood up. Adele noted the tag clipped to the front pocket of his short-sleeved, olive-colored dress shirt indicated his name was Carl. He had been the primary night shift custodian at the university library for nearly twenty years, a time which was an education unto itself regarding the best and worst aspects of college student behavior. He ran an age-spotted hand across the thin strands of white hair that partially covered his forehead and then tucked a corner of his shirt back into the dark jeans he wore.

"Did you get a look at the man who ran by you?"

Carl glared at Adele, clearly annoyed by the question.

"No, I didn't, because I couldn't see his damn face. He was wearing one of those hoodie things."

Carl glanced into the gloom that was the archive room's interior and scowled.

"Why is it so dark in there?"

He then took a moment to look at Adele more carefully before shaking his head in a show of disgust.

"Never mind, I think I figured it out. You young folks these days suffer from too many hormones and not enough sense. Having a private moment in a public library, eh? Wouldn't be the first time I'd interrupted something like that, and most likely won't be the last. Now why don't you get yourself on out of here young lady? I'm sure your boyfriend is waiting for you outside."

Adele's eyes widened at the description.

"He was a young man? The guy you just saw run out of here, he was my age?"

Carl shook his head again.

"I told you, I don't know. I just assumed. He was strong though; I'll give him that. Pushed me into this wall here easy enough. Maybe if you had the light on in there, I would have gotten a better look at him. Then again, I'm guessing that light was off for a reason."

It was then that Carl, himself a father of two daughters and four granddaughters, realized how rattled Adele actually was. His annoyance quickly transformed into concern for the female college student standing in front of him.

"Hey, was that man bothering you? Do you want me to call campus security?"

Adele shook her head while she readjusted her backpack on her shoulders.

"No, I'm fine, thank you. Are you sure you didn't see his face?"

This time Carl's expression was one of regret instead of annoyance.

"I'm sorry, no. I just couldn't see him, and it all happened so fast."

Adele flinched as the sound of her cell phone echoed against the concrete walls. It was her newspaper editor, T.J. Levine. T.J. worked as an investigative reporter in Seattle for nearly thirty years. After retiring from the newspaper business, he accepted a position at the university three years ago to supervise the college newspaper. As the faculty editor, he was tough but fair. His opinions were based on first-hand experience in the business, and that meant a great deal to Adele.

T.J. told Adele that Decklan Stone's publicist had called an hour earlier to schedule a follow-up interview with the author next week. Adele, still shaken from the brief encounter with the stranger, failed to immediately respond.

"Adele, are you there? I figured you'd be a bit more excited about this. You got a call back from a guy whose last interview took place before you were even born!"

Adele cleared her throat while Carl the custodian continued to look at her like a concerned grandfather.

"Thanks for the good news, T.J. I have a favor to ask though."

"Oh, what is it?" T.J. said with cautious curiosity.

"I want to make a trip to the islands again before I meet with Mr. Stone. There are some parts of the story I want to look into."

T.J. knew the sound of a reporter chasing a potential story well enough to realize he could do little to dissuade Adele from proceeding with her plan, regardless of what he said.

"What story is that?"

"Decklan Stone, his wife's death, something happened in those islands, T.J., I can feel it. Something that was left unsaid, covered up, I'm not sure exactly. I just know it."

"Adele, you're to be conducting an interview, *not an investigation*. There is a significant difference between those two things."

"I'm going where the story is leading me."

Adele was proving her editor right—she wasn't going to be dissuaded.

"When are you leaving?" he asked.

"First thing tomorrow, I'll be going to Roche Harbor to speak with a woman there."

"So, what's the favor?"

"I was hoping you could let my professors know that I'll be away for a few more days on a newspaper assignment."

T.J. already suspected that was only part of the favor Adele was requesting.

"Is that it?"

"And I'm going to need some money to cover expenses. The ferry ride, food, transportation, the basics."

Adele could hear her editor shaking his head over the phone.

"You know we're already running this paper on fumes, Adele, and now I'm supposed to explain to the department why I'm sending reporters on multiple paid trips to the San Juan Islands?"

"Yes."

T.J. couldn't help chuckling. Adele's enthusiasm, her pursuit of that unknown truth that drove all good reporters, was a reminder of his own idealistic beginnings as a journalist.

"Okay, Adele, I'll have the funds ready for you to pick up in the office tomorrow morning, so long as you can do me favor as well."

"Sure, what is it?"

T.J. paused. Over the years, he had seen colleagues lose themselves to the pursuit of the unknown only to be devoured by the process and ending up little more than empty shells of their former selves.

"Please be careful."

8.

The ferry ride back to the islands via the terminal in Anacortes was a leisurely journey that allowed Adele a second chance to more fully appreciate the stunning beauty of that part of the world. By the time the ferry navigated the access ramp in Friday Harbor, the small urban hub of the San Juan Islands, Adele was only mildly surprised to find herself enjoying a sense of having returned to a place she could easily call home, even though it was only her second time coming to the islands.

Adele spent some the ferry ride reviewing the photographs from the magazine feature on Decklan and Calista Stone that she had taken with her following the scare in the basement of the university library. She stared into the eyes of the young couple and tried to imagine what each of them were like before tragedy ended the life of one, and forever altered the life of the other.

As Adele walked off the large, white-hulled, three-story ferry and onto the streets of Friday Harbor, a satisfied smile was already spreading across her face. The air had just a hint of a chill, though the morning sun already indicated the spring day was going to be an unusually warm one. The ferry traffic descended upon the small, island town like eager locusts desperate to soak up as much of the island's unique personality as quickly as possible.

Adele chose to take a slower, more deliberate approach as she imagined both Decklan and Calista Stone arriving at this very same location three decades earlier. They were two East Coast transplants enjoying the benefits of an international bestseller and thus the means to then live where they so desired.

They chose here, she thought.

The town of Friday Harbor rose up on a hillside that overlooked the confluence of water, rock, and sand, offering an escape suitable for almost anyone seeking it out. It was a place that felt both old and new, with a playful charm magnified by colorful storefronts and the smiles of tourists and locals as they mingled in a symbiotic dance unique to places such as this.

Adele readjusted her backpack and began the journey up the hill from the ferry terminal to the main road that bisected the center of Friday Harbor's primary business district. Prior to leaving Bellingham, she had looked up the bookstore's address. It was the very same bookstore Calista Stone had visited on the day of her death.

After a ten-minute walk, Adele spotted the sign located across the street from where she stood that signaled she had reached her initial investigative destination—Island Books.

A smaller sign hanging inside the front door indicated the bookstore was open. The building's faded green exterior was cracked and peeling, clearly in need of a fresh coat of paint. A small, concrete marker on the lower left portion of the building's foundation communicated its original date of construction as 1949.

Adele waited for a slow-moving delivery truck to pass in front of her before she walked across the street and then stood just outside the bookstore entrance looking in through the large glass window that dominated the storefront. She could see rows of shelves stuffed with paperback books but couldn't tell if anyone was actually inside. If they were, they were hidden from view.

A single bell hanging over the entrance signaled Adele's arrival. A middle-aged woman strode from the back of the store to give Adele a welcoming smile. Her short, curly hair framed her blue eyes and friendly, lightly lined face. She was of medium height and build, smelled of patchouli and strong coffee, and wore an oversized, dark red sweater and loose-fitting khaki slacks with a pair of white, orthopedic tennis shoes.

"Hello there! Are you looking for anything in particular or just browsing?"

Adele returned the woman's smile.

"My name is Adele Plank. I work for the college newspaper in Bellingham."

The store owner's eyes widened slightly, as did her smile.

"Nice to meet you, Adele. My name is Suzanne Blatt, but everyone just calls me Suze."

Adele glanced at the thousands of books organized in a rather reckless fashion throughout the store and then cleared her throat.

"I'm doing a story, an interview, with the author, Decklan Stone."

Suze's eyes widened further as she pointed back at Adele.

"*You're* the college girl interviewing the writer! Everyone is talking about it! Oh, my goodness, how wonderful that you stopped by. Please follow me and let's sit down and have a talk. I just made a fresh pot of coffee. Can I pour you a cup?"

Adele mumbled her thanks as she followed the woman across the scuffed and unvarnished wood floor into a partially enclosed area at the very back of the store that contained a rectangular white table, two matching chairs, and an aged *Mr. Coffee* that sat next to an old and badly chipped porcelain sink.

"If you need to use the bathroom, it's right over there."

Suze pointed to a narrow hallway located in the far-corner of the small space.

"Did you say you wanted some coffee?"

Adele nodded.

"That would be nice, thank you."

Suze took one of four mismatched coffee cups that were scattered across the small wood countertop adjacent to the sink and then proceeded to pour it from the off-white coffee machine that appeared to have been purchased in the 1970s.

"Do you take anything with your coffee, Adele?" Suze asked.

"Just a little sugar," Adele answered.

A moment later and Suze was seated at the small table across from Adele, sipping from her coffee cup with a smile that seemed to nearly each of her ears.

"How wonderful it must be to have an opportunity to interview a writer like Decklan Stone. My mother was very good friends with his wife. In fact, wait here, I have something to show you."

Suze rose from her chair and disappeared into the main area of the bookstore while Adele took a drink from her cup and found its contents to be a particularly rich and pleasing brew.

"Here, look at this," Suze said upon her return.

Adele took the small black and white photo into her hands and found herself staring at an image of Calista Stone sitting in the very chair and table that Adele was using. Calista, and another woman who appeared somewhat older, were staring back at the camera with two cups of coffee in front of them. The other woman was dark-haired and slightly overweight.

"That's my mother with the writer's wife, Calista. The picture was taken the very same day Calista died. My mom kept it safe all those years after. They really were the best of friends. Of course, my mother said Calista was friends with *everyone*. That was just her nature. She didn't have a mean bone in her body, and she always found time to make people feel welcome and appreciated. Nobody deserved to die the way she did, but someone like her, well, it just makes it that much more tragic I suppose."

Suze leaned in closer to Adele from across the table.

"And if anyone tries to tell you the writer had anything to do with his wife's death, don't you believe it. Mom made that very clear to me, and more than once. Decklan loved Calista with all his heart. I imagine it's why he's never remarried. A love like that, well, it just never ends even after one of those involved is gone. That's how I like to think of it, anyways. I suppose it's all the love stories I enjoy reading."

"Have you met him? Mr. Stone?"

Suze took another sip as she nodded.

"The writer? Yes, but just once since I took over the store after my mother passed away. That was about, oh, six or seven years ago. He came in wearing a baseball cap. I think he thought it might keep his identity hidden. That might work for most of the people around here, but not me. I knew who he was as soon as he walked through that door. Such a handsome man. He didn't say anything at first, just sort of wandered about the store looking at books, thumbing through the pages. I eventually worked up the courage to ask him if he would sign my poor old, dog-eared copy of *Manitoba*."

Adele found herself being completely drawn into Suze's version of having met Decklan Stone, sharing much of the older woman's enthusiasm for him.

"Now that seemed to rattle him just a bit, but then he shrugged and said sure. I ran and got my copy and handed it to him with a pen and he signed it just like I asked. He has beautiful penmanship. Then he bought a copy of *Dante's Inferno*, complimented me on my selection of books, and left. I snuck a peek at him through the window, watched him make his way down the street, and just like that, he disappeared. He hasn't been back in since, though, I've had people tell me from time to time they've seen him around. Apparently, he has a little boat he uses quite often to visit all of the islands.

"Do you think that was the reason he came here, to just get a copy of *Dante's Inferno*?"

Suze shook her head.

"No, not at all. I *know* why he came here. It wasn't to buy a book. It was to experience a place he knew his wife loved to visit. He wanted to see the world through her eyes so as not to forget her. He's trying to keep her memory alive because if he fails to do that, he will have lost her twice."

Suze's remark had Adele reaching into her backpack for a pen and paper.

"Is it okay if I write that down? I'd like to use it for the article."

The bookstore owner appeared genuinely humbled by the request as her mouth opened, closed, and then opened again.

"*Really*? You think it's good enough for something like that? I mean, if you want, sure, go ahead."

Adele finished scribbling down the remark.

"It's definitely quote-worthy, trust me."

"Suze's face colored with a subtle blush.

"I don't think I've ever been quoted before. It's quite an honor."

Suddenly Suze's eyes widened again.

"Say, are you going to be speaking to Delroy Hicks while you're here?"

The name wasn't familiar to Adele.

"Who?"

Suze rose from her chair to refill her cup. Adele placed a hand over her own cup to indicate she didn't want any more coffee.

"He's a writer as well, research mostly. He lives on this beautiful old sailboat over in Roche Harbor. Comes in here about once a month to donate books. He *always* has books to give away. The man must read a hundred or more a year. Anyway, Delroy and Decklan Stone are acquaintances I guess you could say. Birds of a feather sticking together and all that. He's dropped Decklan's name in casual conversation with me from time to time over the years."

Suze lowered her voice even though there was no-one else but Adele and her in the bookstore. Her eyes darted from side to side.

"And he's a homosexual."

Adele stifled the urge to laugh at the older woman's hushed, secretive sharing of another person's sexual preference.

"And you don't think this Mr. Hicks would mind talking with me?"

Suze flipped her hand toward Adele.

"Delroy? Oh, heavens no. That one loves to talk. I have his number and can give him a call right now if you like."

Adele nodded.

"Thank you. That would be great."

The store owner made her way to the front counter to use the landline phone. While she was away, Adele took a moment to look up Delroy Hicks on her cell phone and discovered he was a relatively well-known author of Northwest Native American history with nine titles to his name, including significant contributions to three textbook editions, and had been a regular paid guest lecturer for a number of years on the college campus lecture circuit. He was born in Ireland seventy-two years ago and came to America as a young man with his parents in the 1960s during the Kennedy years. From there he graduated high school in Boston and then attended the University of Washington on an academic scholarship.

Adele grinned to herself as she heard Suze's voice whisper in her head while she finished reading Delroy's bio off of her phone.

And he's a homosexual.

"Okay, it's all set. You'll find his boat on E-Dock, Slip twenty-two. He said to stop on by anytime this afternoon. Just ring the bell and he'll be right out to greet you. Do you have a car?"

Adele shook her head.

"No, but I can just call a taxi."

Suze appeared horrified by the thought.

"Oh, no, that won't be necessary. It's lunchtime anyways. I'll drive you over to Roche Harbor myself. It'll give us a chance to talk some more."

Adele was about to decline the offer, but Suze made clear she wasn't having it.

"Nope, not another word. My mind is made up. Is there anyone else you planned on interviewing here on the island?"

Adele considered saying no, but then thought better of it. She saw no need to keep secrets from someone who had so willingly just given her more information and another interview lead.

"Yes, the owner of the Roche Harbor Hotel."

Suze whirled around after hanging the *Out to Lunch* sign on the store's front door.

"You're going to try and speak with Tilda? Well, good luck with *that*!"

"What do you mean?"

Suze appeared to want to say something, struggled with potentially doing so, and then apparently thought better of it.

"You'll see. She's not the same woman she once was. It's been a gradual but steady regression, but to those of us who remember how she was before, well, she's different now—very different."

"Different good or different bad?" Adele asked.

A shadow of sad reflection passed over Suze's features.

"You'll see. Your best chance of speaking with her is to ask the hotel manager, Phillip. He's a very nice young man, but also protective of Tilda. A big part of his duties is trying to keep her away from potential trouble. I imagine these days it's pretty much a full-time job. It's certainly a job I think few could perform as well as he has."

Suze's near-permanent smile and sunny disposition quickly returned.

"Ready to go?"

Adele nodded, not entirely sure where, or more accurately, *what* she was going to. She sensed the mystery that was slowly unfolding before her. With each person she spoke to, yet another layer of that mystery was revealed. She hoped that eventually the truth might finally be known. If some of that truth was to be found in Roche Harbor, then to Roche Harbor she would go.

9.

The car ride to Roche Harbor was especially pleasant, with ample amounts of sunshine accompanying the way there and Suze happily pointing out various points of interest on the island. Adele was surprised at how the tree-dotted, tall-grassed valleys of San Juan Island's interior contrasted its famously rocky, saltwater shores.

And then she saw something most unexpected. It was a fully-grown camel standing inside a fenced field, watching the cars as they passed by.

"Was that a...?"

Suze's head fell back against the car seat as she laughed at her passenger's disbelief.

"Your eyes aren't lying, young lady. That there is our resident camel, Millie. She's been here almost ten years now. You should see all the tourists when they see her. They point and shout and then out come the cameras!"

Suze appeared capable of driving her Honda from Friday Harbor to Roche Harbor blindfolded. She turned, braked, and accelerated with practiced ease, having navigated the stretch of road thousands of times over the years.

"The grass looks so dry out here, even in the spring."

Suze nodded.

"Lot of folks don't realize how much less rain we get than say, Seattle or Bellingham. I've heard it called the rain shadow, or the Sunbelt, but I just prefer to think of it as a place that has a lot of nice weather. What clouds do roll in don't tend to stay long. And the winter months bring the storm watchers who love to sit inside a beachfront cabin with a nice cup of coffee or glass of wine and watch the wind, lightning, and sea put on some spectacular performances."

A single brown rabbit darted across the road. Suze pointed the car to the left, corrected quickly and returned to her lane as if the effort was as natural to her as breathing.

"Lots of those critters around here. Keeps the hawks, eagles and foxes well fed, I'll tell you that. When I was a girl, men would come from all over the mainland to hunt them. We had thousands and thousands of those rabbits running around all over this island."

"Yeah, but a camel?"

Suze laughed again.

"Hey, I'm not rich by a long shot, but if I were, and could live anywhere in the world, this would be the place I'd choose. The water, the fields, and the people—my goodness, the people! We're an interesting bunch, that's for sure. And along with all the natural beauty, there's a mystery to the islands. You feel it in your bones. Over the years I've watched so many different faces get off those ferries and look around and then just shake their heads because they can't believe how beautiful and different these islands truly are. We have the water, the rocks, the trees, the tall grasses, and even some places in the interior that look like a kind of desert. It's as if God shook the paint brush and then looked down at a perfectly wonderful and contradictory result, and just let it all be."

Adele glanced at Suze who appeared completely unaware of just how profound her words were.

"You did it again."

Suze scowled as she looked over at Adele.

"Did what?"

"Said something I might end up using in my article."

Suze rolled her eyes and shook her head.

"Stop it. You're just being nice. Hey, look down there."

Adele was greeted by a glimpse of shimmering blue water and the metallic glimmer of rows of sailboat masts peeking out from between clusters of tall evergreen trees. The little car followed the considerable descent of the narrow, paved road and then Adele's eyes widened at the image that was laid out before her.

It was the Roche Harbor resort in all its seemingly timeless, Victorian-era glory.

"I'll drop you off in front of the General Store. Just head on down the main dock until you come to E-Dock on the left and it's just a short walk from there to Slip 22. Delroy is already expecting you, so as I said earlier, just ring the bell and he'll be right on out. Oh, and remember that if you still want to try and speak with Tilda at the hotel, you'll want to see Phillip first. He's usually somewhere around the front desk during regular business hours."

Adele let herself out of the passenger seat and then turned around to see Suze already walking toward her with outstretched arms.

"Now you come here and give this old girl a hug. This made for a bit of excitement and I'm always up for some of that when I can get it."

After the brief hug, Adele gave Suze a grateful smile.

"Thank you so much for all the information and the ride here. I'll be sure to stop in and say hello the next time I'm in Friday Harbor."

Suze wagged her finger.

"You better. And make sure to take some time to enjoy this place. It really is very special. I'm sure Delroy will help with that. He's a *very* interesting man."

Adele watched Suze drive away. She honked her horn just before the vehicle disappeared behind the trees. Adele turned around to take in more completely the expansive property that was Roche Harbor. A red-bricked path led to a long walkway covered by flowering vines and at the other end of that path Adele arrived at the hub of the harbor community. To her right was a large two-story restaurant painted white with green trim which was the identical color of the other original buildings that dominated the resort facility. A large outdoor eating space overlooked the pristine marina waters below.

It's like a postcard come to life.

On Adele's left was an even larger white and green-trimmed building that housed a food and supplies store and another restaurant, while directly in front of her was the large wooden dock that led to the marina facility below. Several multi-million-dollar luxury yachts sat in their slips. There were smaller boats as well, lending the place an interesting mix of those with great wealth and those of much more humble means who simply enjoyed spending whatever time they could on the water.

The summer crowds were still a month away, so many of the marina's slips were vacant, and the assorted docks and walkways were not nearly as crowded as they would soon be. Adele used her phone to take several photos and then remembered she hadn't yet located the hotel.

Only after turning all the way around did she discover it looming directly behind her on the other side of the covered walk path. Like the other Roche Harbor buildings, it too was white and green, and had a second-floor balcony that extended the entire front length of the structure. It reminded Adele of something out of an American western film from the 1950s. The hotel, though having maintained its original rustic nature, was also a majestic thing that was an undeniable reminder of the area's storied, 19th Century history.

Adele took a deep breath and was delighted to be greeted by the multiple scents of freshly bloomed flowers, saltwater, and the mouth-watering aroma of food cooking inside the nearby restaurants.

A short walk on a path took Adele to the small dockside restaurant she had spotted earlier. She marveled at how meticulously clean the surroundings were, from the red bricks to the wood docks, and the gorgeous hanging baskets of flowers in the midst of their spring awakening. She walked up to the counter at the restaurant and was greeted by a smiling, middle-aged man dressed in a white golf shirt, blue jeans, and a red baseball cap from which a long brown ponytail protruded. His longish face was lightly covered with salt-and-pepper whiskers and a pair of round glasses.

"Hey there—get you something?"

The man's voice was somewhat high-pitched and friendly.

"What do you recommend? This is my first time here."

The man folded his arms and looked Adele up and down.

"Hmm, you look like a fish and chips type to me. We make 'em right here."

Adele gave a quick nod.

"That sounds great, thank you."

The man pointed to the tables and chairs in the restaurant's interior.

"You can take a spot in here or sit at one of the tables outside and I'll bring it to you."

Adele nodded again and looked around the restaurant while the man disappeared into the kitchen. The stained-wood walls were covered in black-and-white photographs that detailed various people and places from around the San Juan Islands. Many were of sailboats and their owners from prior decades who had once called the islands their home.

And then Adele stopped with eyes wide in front of an image located just inside the entrance. It showed Decklan and Calista Stone smiling as they stood in front of the restaurant. Decklan was dressed in a dark suit and tie and Calista was in a flowing satin dress and high heel shoes. Just below the image, almost hidden by the frame, was a bit of dark-ink handwriting:

4th of July Ball, Mr. and Mrs. Stone of New York

Adele grabbed her camera from the back pocket of her jeans and quickly snapped a picture of the photograph.

"Hey, what are you doing?"

Adele turned around and saw the man looking back at her while holding a plate with a sandwich.

"This picture here, do you know the couple?"

The man shrugged. "I know *of* them, sure, but I don't *know* them. That's an old picture that came with the place when I bought it. Why do you ask?"

"I'm doing an interview with the man in the photo, Decklan Stone."

The restaurant owner's eyes widened behind his glasses as he suddenly looked upon Adele with newfound respect.

"Really? You've actually met him, the writer?"

Adelle nodded.

"Yeah."

The man walked toward the entrance door and pointed to a picnic table located in a neatly mowed grass area outside.

"You mind if we sit down out there? The BLT is my treat, no charge. I'm almost out of fish so had to go with something else for you. I hope that was okay."

Adele's stomach growled at the prospect of a free meal. She happily accepted the offer.

"Sure, you lead the way."

A moment later Adele was biting into the most delicious bacon, lettuce, and tomato sandwich she had ever tasted. The toasted dark rye bread was an especially nice touch.

"This is so good!"

The man smiled.

"My name is Bill, by the way. Bill Baldwin."

Adele took another bite of her sandwich, too hungry to care about talking and eating at the same time.

"Nice to meet you, Bill. My name is Adele."

Bill shifted atop the wood bench on his side of the picnic table and paused for a few nervous seconds before proceeding.

"So, do you mind telling me what he's like? I ask because, well, his book, *Manitoba*, it was pretty important to me when I was a young guy struggling to make it to the next day and the story just, it just, uh, it really spoke to me, you know? That picture you were looking at inside my place was one of the reasons I risked everything to buy the business. It was like fate, right? I came here for some downtime and there was Decklan Stone looking at me from his place on that wall. I had a small inheritance after my mom died, had a little chef training from some schooling I took years earlier, and the place had a 'For Sale' sign and so I thought, why not? Six years later and I'm still here. I've been told he lives on a little island of his over in Orcas. People have said he used to come over here to Roche all the time, but he hasn't walked into my restaurant yet. I pretty much gave up hope of that ever happening, but now here you are, someone who has actually met the guy."

Adele swallowed the very last of the BLT, smiled and shrugged.

"Here I am."

Bill chuckled, and then more awkward silence followed before Adele intervened.

"You sure I can't pay for the meal?"

Bill waved away the offer.

"No, but maybe, uh…"

Bill's voice faded before he gathered his courage and finished the thought.

"I was wondering if you could take my copy of *Manitoba* with you and have him sign it."

"That's it?"

Bill issued a soft grunt.

"Well for me that would be quite a lot, actually."

Adele reached across the picnic table.

"You got a deal. It's the least I can do for the free meal, right?"

Bill shook Adele's hand slowly and then leaned forward over the table.

"You think he won't mind?"

Adele withdrew her hand.

"I don't think so. He seems like a pretty nice guy, actually. Quiet, considerate, has that whole mysterious author, hermit-thing going for him."

Bill grunted again.

"Yeah? Wow, that sounds so cool. Wait here, I'll be right back with the book."

Adele watched Bill run into the restaurant and then turned her attention to the rows of flags lined up alongside the wood-planked boardwalk. They fluttered in the soft breeze sweeping across the harbor. Each one represented a different country. She recalled reading online about how the resort would do an elaborate lowering of the flag ceremony at the end of the day during the summer months which included the national anthems of the United States, Canada, and Great Britain. This was followed by raucous cannon fire just as they would have done a century earlier. She hoped to be back during the summer months to witness the ceremony in person.

"Here you go."

Bill handed her his hardcover version of *Manitoba.*

"I'll have him sign it the next time I see him, which should be tomorrow."

Bill's head nodded several times like a cheap plastic, bobble-head doll.

"That would be great, man, just great! So, who are you going to see now? Is it someone around here?"

"Yeah, a guy who lives on a sailboat. And then later I'm hoping to get some time with the owner of the hotel."

Bill grimaced.

"You mean, Tilda?"

Adele noted that the restaurant owner's reaction to Tilda was even more negative than Suze's had been.

"Yes. You seem to think that'll be a problem."

Bill let out a low whistle and glanced behind him to make certain no-one was nearby.

"I don't like to talk about someone who isn't here to defend themselves, but it's no secret around here that the woman is crazy. I'm talking *all out crazy.* Last time I saw her was about six months ago at our monthly merchants meeting. That's when the Roche business owners get together to discuss things like trash collection, painting the storefronts, just little stuff like that. Tilda shows up at the meeting acting weird, making accusations, saying we're all in on the cover up. I was clueless as to what she was talking about, so had to ask around after she left. Nobody wanted to say anything, or they were like me and had no idea what she was talking about. All I *do* know is that she reeked of alcohol, had this look in her eyes like she was ready to kill every one of us at the meeting, and then she just stood up and left, cursing us out the entire time. We could still hear her even when she was walking outside, screaming about the cover-up that was going on."

"And you haven't seen her since that meeting?"

Bill did another quick scan of the area before responding.

"Actually, I did about three weeks ago, but not up close. She was sitting outside on the hotel's second-story balcony looking out at the water. She was like that for most of the day—didn't move from the chair. I walked past in the morning and there she was. I walked by again right before the sun went down, and she was in the exact same spot. I don't even think her eyes were blinking. I heard she still visits the church on the hill sometimes, but I don't go there so I don't know if that's true or not."

Again, Adele extended her hand to shake Bill's.

"Well, I'll let you know how it goes when I bring your book back, hopefully signed. Thank you again for the sandwich. Next time I want to try those fish and chips you promised."

Bill turned around and was halfway inside his restaurant when he looked behind him and shouted at Adele.

"Hey! Who are you going to meet down at the marina?"

Adele looked back with a hand acting as a brim over her eyes to help block out the unexpectedly bright spring sun.

"A guy by the name of Delroy Hicks."

Bill's face broke out into a sly smile which was then replaced by a knowing chuckle as he pointed back at Adele.

"Oh, you're gonna have some fun with that one! You tell the old bastard to get his skinny butt back up here soon. I'm starting to think he's been avoiding me."

Adele watched Bill disappear back into the restaurant and then continued on her way down to the marina and to her meeting with the seemingly well thought of and even more interesting, Delroy Hicks.

10.

The sailboat that occupied Slip 22 was just over thirty feet long with an abundance of varnished wood and gleaming metal. Adele looked up at the aluminum mast that rose upward some forty feet from the vessel's cabin roof and saw a seagull staring back down at her. The white and grey bird issued an unhappy sounding, throaty *awk* noise as a way of greeting and then abruptly flew away.

Adele spotted a brightly polished brass bell hanging out over what she assumed was the vessel's primary entrance into the living space inside. A single string hung from the bottom of the bell's mouth, a device Adele remembered as being called a clapper. She recalled Suze telling her to simply ring the bell once she arrived at the boat and Delroy Hicks would be right out to greet her.

The bell's tone was a deep clang, and its sound initiated an immediate response from inside the boat in the form of a series of loud and angrily hissed curse words.

"Damn it! Damn it! Damn it! Oh, son of a bitch! I've overslept *again*! These constant bloody naps! I'll be right out! Don't go anywhere! I just have to put my teeth in!"

The voice had a hint of an Irish accent and sounded quite panicked as it continued shouting from inside the sailboat.

"Get in there you damn things! Oh, what a travesty this is! Look at them! They don't fit right! I look like a damned fool, all smile and no brains! Pathetic is what I am!"

Adele took a moment to look around, wondering if anyone else could hear the loud complaints as the shouting continued.

"Oh, where is my hat? Where is it? Damn it! Damn it! Damn it! Ah, there she is. Come here, then. Lovely thing. Yes, that's better. I look almost human now. Welcome back to the world of the living, Delroy."

Adele placed her hand over her mouth, trying very hard to stifle a laugh.

The sailboat's door swung open and a thin, mad-eyed little man wearing a light blue fedora with a rainbow-colored ribbon, a simple white dress shirt with the sleeves rolled up, and a pair of blue-and-white-striped cargo shorts, erupted from the boat's bowels. He had a thin, grey beard that didn't quite conceal a set of deeply sunken cheeks that lent him a decidedly emaciated aura as he moved about on shockingly thin, bird-like legs. The ends of his exposed feet were ensconced in a pair of deeply scuffed, leather sandals.

"Ah, you must be Adele."

Despite his thin, sunken-chest frame, Delroy Hicks had one of the most powerful voices Adele had ever heard. While remaining on the boat, he reached out with a thin-fingered hand.

"Hello, Adele. I am Professor Delroy Hicks. If you haven't yet noticed, I'm dying."

Adele's mouth fell open as she found herself shaking Delroy's paper-skin hand while wondering if he was being literal or figurative in explaining his health to a woman he had just met. Delroy then withdrew his hand and used it to remove his hat which exposed a full head of surprisingly thick, grey hair, and with an intentionally dramatic flourish, leaned over at the waist and bowed before his newly arrived guest.

"Welcome to the *No Regrets*."

Adele knew she was unable to hide her confusion. Delroy returned his hat to the top of his head and pointed toward the boat's transom where Adele then saw the name *No Regrets* painted in bold red letters.

"That's her name, and she's all mine. Been living here in this very slip, off and on, for over forty years. Do you know John Wayne was once my guest here? It's true. I cooked him a steak. The man loved steak. He ate two twelve-ounce rib eyes, drank an entire bottle of my best wine, and told stories of his days in old Hollywood. It was a *glorious* affair. He came here somewhat regularly during the summer season on that old World War II ship of his, *The Wild Goose*. He had read my first book on the native tribes of the Pacific Northwest and was a fan. Imagine that—he was a fan of *me*. The man truly gave meaning to the phrase, 'bigger than life.' Even when immersed in his twilight, he was a powerful personality, a fine human being without a hint of Hollywood arrogance. He stood where you are standing now. What do you think of *that*?"

Adele was reeling from information overload and had no idea how to respond. Delroy was either unaware of her confusion, or simply didn't care. He just continued with whatever thought sprang forth from his mile-a-minute mind.

"Suze tells me you're the one who was allowed to interview Decklan. Is that so?"

Adele nodded with her mouth still half open.

Delroy Hicks lifted his head upward and let out a loud, barking laugh.

"Hah, the hermit has finally grown tired of his self-imposed banishment, has he? Well, about bloody time, I'd say. I can't imagine someone with his talent sitting around silently watching the world move by him without a single word on a page to mark its passing. He's an ungrateful prick is what he is, and I love him dearly. So then, what say you, Adele, uh, I'm sorry, what is your last name?"

Adele recovered from her initial confusion enough to respond.

"Plank. It's Adele Plank."

Delroy's eyes appeared to widen almost beyond the orbs that contained them.

"Plank!? Well, isn't that the perfect name for a watery location such as this. We shall call it, *walking the Adele*! So tell me then—what is next for you, Ms. Plank?"

"I'm sorry," Adele replied. "I don't understand."

Delroy extended his arms in front of him and stared across at Adele. His voice lowered an octave further and his green eyes twinkled with delight.

"Do you wish to come aboard?"

Adele's mouth opened further, but no words came out. She found herself completely confused by Delroy Hicks's question.

"I said do you wish to come aboard?" he repeated.

Adele recalled a movie she had seen as a young girl where a Naval officer was visiting a ship from another country where he first had to ask for permission.

Ah, what the hell, she thought. *Give it a try.*

"Permission to come aboard, Mr. Hicks."

Delroy smiled, revealing the oversized dentures he had earlier exclaimed he needed to put in before stepping outside.

"Very good, Ms. Plank. Permission to come aboard has been happily granted."

Adele marveled at how much room there was within the sailboat's stained-wood interior. She was able to stand up fully and look around at a space that included an eating area, a couch, and a small bedroom with an adjoining bathroom.

"This is nice and surprisingly spacious."

Delroy took a seat on one end of the couch and then lightly patted the open space next to him.

"Have to rest a bit, catch my breath. As I said, I *am* dying after all."

Adele removed her backpack and then sat down on the couch as requested.

"Are you *really* dying, Mr. Hicks?"

Delroy's smile collapsed.

"Well, of course I am. That isn't something one goes around saying for the fun of it. Goodness no. It's cancer. I'm absolutely riddled with tumors. Started in my liver and now, well who knows where the damnable things have spread. Last summer they removed a third of my liver and gave me three weeks of radiation treatment and then strongly suggested several sessions of chemotherapy. Not to cure me, mind you, but to potentially extend my life by a year, or possibly two."

Delroy's eyes narrowed and he jabbed a finger into the open air in front of him.

"I said bullshit to that. If you walk to the end of this dock, you'll find a once-beautiful little sailboat now abandoned and nearly as dead as the man who once owned it. His name was Wilfrid. As a younger man he played college football, and even in his sixties was a big, powerfully built sort, yet also a very gentle soul. Three years ago, he was diagnosed. They put him on that poison, and I watched over the months that followed as he wasted away into nothingness. He finally passed shortly before my own diagnosis, and I decided then that I would not make the same mistake he had. What is another year if it's spent unable to get out of bed, or to enjoy a meal, a glass of wine, or to have to watch as every hair on your body falls away? No thank you. I'll let the disease have me, but not the supposed cure."

Delroy suddenly snapped his fingers.

"Ah, that reminds me. It's tea time. Care for a cup?"

Adele silently noted that each of her interviews on the island commenced with the offering of food and drink. She also marveled at Delroy's ability to jump from the subject of his seemingly impending death to making a pot of tea.

"Yes," she said. "Thank you."

Delroy rose from the couch and filled a tea kettle with water from the sink faucet that was the centerpiece of the sailboat's small but functional galley. Then he ignited the flame on one of the two propane burners that made up the cooktop to the right of the sink. He turned halfway around and gave Adele a wink.

"Be just a minute. She warms up fast, just like I used to. In the meantime, tell me something you would like to know about my good friend, the writer."

Adele reached into her backpack and withdrew the recorder.

"Do you mind?"

Delroy shook his head just as the tea pot began to whistle.

"Not at all. It'll give you something to remember me by."

Adele watched as Delroy brought out two white, porcelain teacups and matching saucers. He placed a single tea bag into each cup, filled them with water, and delivered Adele's with a smile and a nod.

"We're drinking rosehip with a touch of black licorice today. I hope you like it."

Delroy returned to his spot on the couch, crossed his skinny legs, took a small sip of tea and then closed his eyes and grinned.

"Oh, yes, that's the ticket. So, Ms. Plank, give us something to talk about before this gets painfully awkward. Not that I mind awkward. That can be fun too."

Adele wondered if Delroy's overtly friendly nature was in fact a way for him to constantly be talking without saying anything, so she decided to open with the very question that seemed to divide those on the islands who knew about Decklan Stone and his long-ago deceased wife.

"Do you think he killed her?"

Delroy took another sip of tea, seemingly unfazed. He gave a shrug of his bony shoulders and then cleared his throat.

"Before approaching that kind of question, one should first ask if Decklan was even capable of actually *doing* such a thing. I knew them well but knew Decklan perhaps more than anyone else other than his wife. Calista was outgoing to the point where she seemed almost desperate for approval, whereas Decklan's personality has always been far more introverted. You had to have patience to get to the man behind the myth. Ah, but what success he was. Imagine being as young as that and having the *New York Times*, the *Boston Globe*, *LIFE*, all of them singing the praises of this new American author. Decklan swam in those waters for a bit and found them too deep, too cold, and all too dangerous to the well-being of his marriage. Was he capable of murder?"

Delroy paused to drink the last of his tea and then continued. Adele sat listening, fully enthralled by the big voice coming from the little man who sat beside her.

"Yes, of course, we are all capable of such things when placed in the right, or should I say, the wrong circumstances. But of the two, I would still wager it would be Calista who was more capable of doing such a thing. She was a jealous, possessive woman, perpetually battling her feelings of both pride and insecurity regarding her husband's sudden success. If an attractive woman were to make her way toward Decklan, Calista's claws would come out. And it was Decklan who was most often left with the scratch of his wife's jealousy. That is not to say her fears were without merit. Decklan created a bit of a reputation when he was in New York, but upon his arrival here, there was no evidence to suggest he was anything less than an utterly devoted husband."

"What about Tilda?"

Delroy's brows rose slightly at the mention of the hotel owner who was among the last to see Calista Stone alive.

"Ah, Tilda-Tilda-Tilda. She's not nearly so lost as some around here would believe."

"How well do you know her?"

Delroy grimaced and then reached down to touch his side.

"Are you okay?" Adele asked.

Delroy gave a short nod and then groaned.

"It'll pass. I just need a minute."

Adele watched as Delroy took several deep breaths and then cleared his throat.

"Apologies, these pains are getting more frequent of late. Now, where were we?"

"I asked you how well you knew Tilda."

Delroy placed his teacup and saucer on the galley counter. Then he folded his arms across his chest and seemed to be looking up at something Adele couldn't see.

"Yes, Tilda, a rather complicated subject, that. As far as my knowing her, I know her enough to have had dinner with her just two nights earlier in her private residence at the hotel. We are among the longest-term Roche Harbor residents, you see. The trick with her is to ignore the past because it's the past that's killing her as surely as this cancer is killing me."

"Please explain what that means."

Delroy stood up and pointed to the sailboat's open door.

"Could we have a walk and talk? I try to keep moving as much as possible and today's weather is especially warm for this time of year, and I'd like to enjoy it, if that's okay."

Adele joined Delroy outside on the dock and was soon walking alongside him as he continued to share his knowledge of the mystery surrounding Decklan and Calista Stone and Tilda's place within that same story.

"There are two things to understand regarding Tilda Ashland. One, she blames herself for causing the argument that led to Calista's death. Two, she is convinced Decklan did in fact kill his wife and that the murder was subsequently covered up by the local authorities, namely by the former San Juan County Sheriff, Martin Speaks."

Adele stopped walking and turned to face Delroy.

"I met the sheriff in Deer Harbor. He came off rather…"

Delroy was already nodding his head.

"Like a complete asshole? Yes, he is. And he absolutely detests me. Rather homophobic, that one. What did he have to say to you?"

The two began walking again to the end of another of several docks that extended out over the Roche Harbor waters.

"He basically told me not to go back for another interview with Decklan Stone, and he was pretty aggressive about it too. Thankfully the woman who owns the store over there intervened and got him away from me."

"Oh, you mean Bella."

Adele nodded.

"She's a fine lady, isn't she? My goodness I haven't seen her in, it must be three, perhaps four, years. Do you have idea why the sheriff didn't want you talking with Decklan?"

A seal's glossy black head broke the surface of the water no more than forty feet from where Adele and Delroy stood on the dock. The sea mammal appeared to be waiting for Adele's answer as much as Delroy was.

"No, not really."

Delroy stared at Adele. He seemed to sense she had more to tell, and that she required just a bit of gentle prodding to do so.

"What is it?" he asked.

Adele noted how he had somehow become the one interviewing her.

"I thought I was supposed to be the person asking the questions?"

Delroy grinned as he stroked his beard.

"Ah, you noticed that did you? It's just my nature, always brushing away the dirt to see what is found just beneath the surface."

"And why is that?"

Delroy trapped Adele's eyes in his own and held them there for a moment before responding.

"Because, my dear girl, that is so often where the truth resides. Now turn around and look behind you."

Adele paused, made certain she wasn't standing too close to the water, and then did as Delroy requested.

"Look up toward the hill," he continued.

Adele saw the upper half of the Roche Harbor hotel.

"Do you see her? She's watching us. She's *always* watching what goes on down here. It's her nature, and an animal rarely changes its fundamental nature."

At the center of the hotel's second-story balcony stood a woman dressed in a loose-fitting white dress that hung down to her ankles. And though Adele couldn't see her face, she knew who the woman was.

Tilda.

"Now that she's seen you with me, your chances of being able to meet with her tonight have vastly improved."

Adele turned. "You met with me for *her* benefit?"

Delroy frowned.

"No, Ms. Plank, I did it for *your* benefit, yours and Decklan's."

The seal remained floating just beyond the dock, watching their conversation.

"I don't understand."

Delroy removed his hat and ran a hand through his thick shock of grey hair and then returned the hat to its perch atop his head.

"I think you do. It's why you're here speaking with me. It's why you want to try and talk with Tilda. It's why you took time to stop in at the bookstore and have coffee with Suze. And it's why you're willing to risk the anger of someone like Sheriff Speaks."

"Okay, Mr. Hicks, please tell me why it is I'm doing these things."

Delroy leaned in close to Adele and whispered his answer into her ear.

"For the mystery, my young friend. The mystery!"

11.

"I'm sorry, Ms. Ashland is not available. Would you like a room?"

Phillip Ozere was a tall, slightly overweight man in his early forties. He was dressed in a crisp, white shirt, red tie, and black dress slacks. He regarded Adele with a formal indifference, as if his position at the Roche Harbor Hotel was comparable to being the official greeter of Buckingham Palace. His fleshy cheeks were riddled with pockmarks, likely the byproduct of especially bad skin during his youth.

"Suze indicated you might be willing to ask her for me, and I'm also an acquaintance of Mr. Delroy Hicks."

Phillip's features softened, and he took another moment to look Adele up and down.

"You know Suze?"

"Yes, I spent the day with her. I'm a reporter for the college newspaper in Bellingham. I just want to ask Ms. Ashland a few questions."

Phillip's guarded demeanor quickly returned.

"A reporter? No, I don't think that will be possible. And now that I've checked, it doesn't appear we have any rooms available, either."

Adele rose to her full height, a less than impressive five-foot-four, and gave the hotel manager an exaggerated shrug.

"Well, I'm sorry to hear that. You leave me with no choice but to note that Ms. Ashland made no comment on the subject in my article. This will, of course, lead to speculation among readers and might harm the reputation of the hotel."

Phillip's eyes narrowed.

"What subject are you talking about?"

Adele shook her head.

"I'm afraid that is between me and the owner of this hotel."

Adele could see Phillip struggling with the decision. His loyalty to Tilda was clearly evident. After several seconds, with Phillip standing behind the massive oak desk that dominated the hotel's red-and-gold-carpeted lobby, he issued a final answer.

"I am going to ask you to leave. Now."

Adele looked around the lobby, confirming she and Phillip were the only ones there. To her right was the wide staircase leading to the second floor and the guest rooms. Adele knew that somewhere up there she would find Tilda.

"I tell you what, Phillip, I'm going to wait over there in one of those nice chairs next to that big stone fireplace and give you a chance to reconsider, okay?"

Before Phillip could respond, Adele walked quickly across the wood plank floor and sat down in one of two high-backed, green upholstered chairs that faced what appeared to be the hotel's original limestone fireplace mantel. She removed a paper pad from her backpack and pretended to write notes in it. The lobby, being lit by just a few antique lamps placed in various corners of the large room, was being overtaken by late-day shadow.

C'mon, Phillip, Adele thought, *at least go up there and ask her.*

Phillip remained standing, utterly immobile, behind the lobby desk. Adele could feel his eyes boring into her back.

It was a sitting standoff.

I'm just going to stay right here. He can stand over there glaring at me all he wants.

Nearly an hour went by before Adele heard the sound of footsteps as a likely guest entered the hotel lobby from outside. She glanced at her phone and noted it was nearly seven-thirty. Darkness had settled over Roche Harbor.

The footsteps didn't make their way to the lobby desk, though. Instead, they indicated someone was approaching the very chair Adele was sitting in. By the time Adele moved to turn her head and see who it was, the person was sitting down in the other chair directly across from her.

Adele's mouth dropped open, and she let out a soft gasp.

The hard gaze of Tilda Ashland settled upon Adele.

"You wish to speak with me?"

Adele, caught off guard, initially stammered, forced herself to focus, and then responded.

"Yes, my name is Adele Plank. I believe you saw me speaking with Delroy earlier."

Tilda smiled, showing a row of age-yellowed teeth. Her skin was remarkably smooth for a woman of nearly sixty, and her shoulder-length red hair remained almost as long and luxurious as it had been during the days of her youth, with just a hint of grey showing amidst its thick strands. The fingers were strong yet also delicate, and the legs underneath the white lace dress she wore appeared to be as well. Adele looked at Tilda's chest and then quickly glanced away, only to find herself drawn back again.

A swath of translucent lace covered the upper portion of Tilda's dress. She wasn't wearing a bra and the material was not nearly opaque enough to hide her ample breasts and the dark outline of her nipples.

"Yes, I saw you speaking with Delroy. That's the only reason I'm willing to speak with you now."

Tilda leaned back and extended her hand. Phillip placed a nearly full glass of amber-hued whiskey into it. She took a long, slow drink, emptying a third of the contents.

"Tell me what you want from me, but don't you dare lie, little girl. I have no patience for lies."

Adele could smell the hotel owner's alcohol-drenched breath and marveled at how Tilda was able to function given the amount she already appeared to have consumed.

"I'm doing an interview with the writer, Decklan Stone."

Tilda's eyes flickered ice, and her cold smile sent a shiver down Adele's spine.

"I am quite certain I'm not Decklan Stone. You appear to be speaking to the wrong person."

"I know you were friends with both Decklan and Calista, and—"

Tilda hissed and then looked away for a moment as if trying to recall something she had long ago forgotten. The drink remained clasped in her hand, while the tips of her other hand's nails dug into the chair's arm.

"You don't know *anything*," she seethed.

Though shaken by Tilda's obvious instability, Adele was determined to forge ahead, not certain that she would ever be given the opportunity to speak with her again.

"I know what Decklan told me of that day, and then the night that Calista died. He mentioned you and that is what brought me here. I wanted to hear *your* version. I wanted to show you that respect."

Tilda's mouth curled into a grotesque, savage snarl. The words she spoke next were spit out like a cobra striking upon its frightened prey.

"Decklan Stone is a killer. A murderer. Don't talk to me of respect. Don't talk to me of Calista. You. Know. Nothing."

Tilda brought the glass to her mouth and proceeded to empty its contents in a single swallow. It was then flung into the fireplace where it shattered in much the same way it seemed Tilda's life had been shattered when Calista Stone forever sank beneath dark waters twenty-seven-years earlier.

Phillip rushed to Tilda's side and gently placed a hand onto her shoulder.

"Ms. Ashland, we do have guests."

Tilda appeared ready to scream at Phillip as well, but then she saw movement from the second floor as an older woman looked out from a partially open door. The hotel owner let out a deep, exhausted sigh and then pointed toward the lobby desk. Her words were slightly slurred as her chin fell onto her chest.

"Bring me another drink."

Phillip whispered into Tilda's ear.

"Perhaps it's best you retire for the evening, Ms. Ashland."

Tilda closed her eyes and began to chuckle. Her response arrived softly at first, but then grew in volume with each subsequent word spoken.

"Thank you for your concern, Phillip. Now do as you're told and *get me another drink.*"

Phillip stood up again, paused, and then finally surrendered with a curt nod.

"Yes, Ms. Ashland, right away."

Tilda's eyes opened slowly until she was looking at Adele.

"What was the reason Delroy sent you? What part is he playing in this?"

Adele shook her head.

"I'm not sure what you mean."

"Yes, you are. Stop playing games. Clearly, he wanted you here, and I'm now demanding you tell me why."

Tilda's volatile nature made it difficult for Adele to choose how to answer her question. She chose to simply regurgitate Delroy's own words in the hopes of sounding as truthful as possible.

"He said it would be for my benefit as well as Decklan's."

Phillip returned with the drink. Tilda took it and then pointed to the fireplace.

"Please start a fire, Phillip. I grow cold. It seems I'm always cold anymore."

Phillip quickly set about placing handfuls of kindling onto a pile of old newspaper and then added three large logs atop the pile. Soon the crackle and snap of burning wood echoed throughout the hotel lobby, the fire's light helping to partially push back the shadows from the seating area that housed both Adele and Tilda. Tilda was about to take a sip from her whiskey when she stopped and loudly snapped her fingers together.

"Phillip, bring my guest her own glass, and be quick about it."

Adele was about to decline the offer but then realized it wasn't actually an offer, but in fact an expectation, so she simply waited silently and then accepted the half-full glass of whiskey with a polite, albeit strained, grin.

Tilda gave what appeared to be her first genuine smile since sitting down with Adele.

"Men are good for little, and little good for anyone but themselves, but Phillip is better than most."

Adele took a sip from her glass and tried not to grimace. She had never enjoyed the taste of hard alcohol.

"I'm curious," Tilda said. "Why would Delroy think I, of *all* people, would care about what benefits Decklan?"

Adele found herself once again silently panicked over a question she did not with certainty understand the meaning of. It was clear Tilda blamed Decklan for Calista's death, but Adele was not yet sure if Tilda thought that murder, or merely negligence, was responsible.

"I'm sorry. I don't know. I'm trying to learn more about all of this. I think there is a story here beyond the story that's already been told."

Tilda arched her brows and delivered her second genuine smile of the night.

"Indeed, there is, little girl. No one will listen to me. I'm crazy, you see, which makes me unworthy of being heard—like the old woman in the tower. I am the still-living ghost of Roche Harbor's hidden past, haunting those few who remain alive but choose to forget what happened all those years ago."

Tilda drank from her glass and stared into the flames that licked the air in front of her.

"And now you hope to hear my version as well?"

Adele nodded.

"Yes, I would."

Adele saw Phillip making his way outside. He stopped some ten feet from the hotel entrance and inhaled deeply from a cigarette. Then he blew the smoke out in an angry cloud that swirled around him before dissipating into the darkness. Adele was certain he was looking through one of the large hotel windows to where both women sat talking in front of the fire.

Tilda watched Adele watching Phillip and smiled again, though, this time her eyes were cold and hinted at the madness that lurked just beneath her surface.

"Very well, Adele Plank. I will tell my version. I will tell you what Decklan Stone cannot."

Adele paused with her glass halfway to her lips.

"What version is that?"

The fire's flames danced like wicked children in the depths of Tilda's midnight eyes.

"The truth."

12.

Adele slept far more soundly in one of the sparse but tastefully furnished Roche Harbor Hotel guest rooms than she would have thought possible given the disturbing, decades-long tale that confirmed Tilda Ashland's obsessive certainty that Decklan Stone was guilty of having murdered his wife.

Adele reached across the double bed for her recorder, sat up with her back against the soft, quilted headboard, and pushed play. Tilda's low, slightly slurred voice immediately transported Adele back to the previous night's conversation.

"I saw them arguing. I heard them yelling at one another, but it was the look on his face. It was the look of a man who wanted his wife dead. As soon as I heard she was missing, I knew what Decklan Stone had done. It was no accident. He killed Calista."

"And is that what you told the police?" Adele asked.

Tilda's mouth formed a disgusted frown. She spit out the words as if they were poison.

"Of course, I did. I met with the sheriff personally. He had no use for what I knew. He hardly paid me any attention at all. He *wanted* that case to be over. He's a lazy, worthless little man. That gun on his hip was always just for show. And then who is it hired by Decklan to bring him supplies to his island but the man's own simple-minded son. Coincidence? I think not."

Adele reached down and turned the volume of her recorder up and then closed her eyes as she tried to relive every nuance of the conversation.

"And this was Sheriff Speaks, correct?"

Tilda sniffed.

"Yes, the arrogant bastard. I went back again to ask why the case had been closed so quickly. He ignored me. Then he warned me to stop harassing him, said he would get a restraining order if needed."

The recording indicated a long, silent break in the conversation before Tilda continued. By then she sounded tired, spent well beyond her nearly sixty years.

"It was as if he wanted Calista buried and gone from everyone's memory, as if she had never been at all. I didn't forget though. I will *never* forget."

Adele pushed pause on the recorder, withdrew a pen and notepad, and wrote down Tilda's comment. She didn't know yet why those words were so significant, but she was certain they hinted at something important, something right in front of her.

Something she was missing.

I've got to get moving, she thought. *I'll finish reviewing the interview when I get back to Bellingham.*

Adele washed, brushed her teeth, and changed into fresh clothes. She put her shoulder-length hair into a ponytail, and in less than fifteen minutes from getting out of bed, was walking down the hotel staircase and on her way outside.

"Good morning, Ms Plank. I trust you slept well?"

Adele stopped at the lobby desk behind which Phillip stood looking exactly as he had the day before.

"Yes, thank you. Is Ms. Ashland up yet? I'd like to tell her thanks for giving me a free stay here."

Phillip's lips pressed tightly together as he shook his head.

"No, Ms. Ashland isn't normally available until later in the day. I will be happy to forward your gratitude to her though."

Adele slapped the top of the desk and headed out the door.

"Thanks, Phillip. You take care."

She was happy to be out of the hotel. Despite the building's considerable size, Adele found its ambiance reflected its owner: unstable, moody, and suffocating.

The walk to Delroy's sailboat was enough to clear away the experience of having met Tilda Ashland. It was a remarkably bright, warm spring morning with just a hint of a breeze and not a single cloud to hinder the blue perfection of the sky.

Adele's footsteps made a heavy, *thunk thunk* as she travelled over the wood dock. More than one stranger looked and gave her a cheerful smile. Once she reached the side of Delroy's boat, Adele rang the bell and waited. When no response came, she rang the bell again.

"Hello? Delroy, are you in there? It's Adele from yesterday."

The sailboat remained still and silent.

What's that smell?

It was the hint of something burning carried on the saltwater breeze. Adele scanned the horizon and saw a pillar of black smoke working across the water from the direction of Orcas Island. She continued to stand and watch the smoke as it expanded like the fingers of a massive, floating hand.

And then a familiar voice sounded from directly behind her, causing Adele to flinch.

"Hello there, Ms. Plank," Decklan said. "I'm sorry, did I scare you?"

Adele shook her head while her eyes drank in the sight of the attractive older man. A thick strand of Decklan's hair hung over his brow and his face was covered in a thin layer of stubble. Decklan wore a pair of faded jeans and a form-fitting, V-neck T-shirt with a pair of ragged, canvas high-top sneakers.

Decklan smelled of gasoline and Adele noted a dark smudge covering the top of his hand.

"You give up writing to be an auto mechanic?"

Decklan appeared confused at first, but then looked down at his hands and chuckled.

"Had a fuel line that needed to be re-clamped on my way over here. Made a bit of a mess."

Adele glanced around.

"You bring your little boat?"

Decklan nodded and pointed toward the end of the dock.

"Yeah, tied up down there. I left early, spent an hour or so walking Sucia, and then made my way here. Figured I'd check in with Delroy, but it looks like he's not around, huh?"

Adele remembered that Sucia was a small island some fifteen miles northeast of Roche Harbor. It was a favorite among beachcombers, noted for its fossilized rocks and multiple coves.

"I guess not."

Decklan took a step forward and cocked his head.

"How do you know Delroy?"

Adele cleared her throat and tried to appear as casual as possible, but knew she was failing miserably.

"I just met him yesterday."

Decklan's eyes widened slightly.

"Uh-huh…"

Adele knew the proverbial jig was up. She had been caught red-handed.

"Okay, yes, I was doing a bit of background on you for the article. I hope that's all right."

Decklan straightened his posture and buried his hands into the back pockets of his jeans.

"So, who else have you talked to besides Delroy?"

Adele glanced up toward the hotel. Decklan, possessing the keen observational powers of a gifted author, noticed immediately. He looked at the hotel and grunted.

"You spoke with Tilda, huh? That must have been a unique experience. Did she convince you I wanted to see Calista dead? That my failure to go to prison is the result of some grand conspiracy?"

Adele stood silent, unable to form a response. Rage flashed briefly across Decklan's face.

"Answer me!" he shouted.

The volume of his demand angered Adele and she found the courage to push back.

"Don't you dare yell at me. I'm a journalist. I'm allowed to speak to whomever I want."

Decklan's rage dissipated just as quickly as it had appeared, and was replaced by his more familiar, polite tone.

"I'm sorry. I shouldn't have spoken to you that way. Seeing you here caught me by surprise is all. I fear I remain overly protective of my privacy. You're correct that I have no right to assume I enjoy any control over those you choose to speak with."

Both Adele and Decklan looked up at the sound of a familiar voice.

"Well-well-well, it is the prodigal friend who has returned. Hello there, Decklan. And a good morning to you as well, Ms. Plank."

Delroy Hicks tilted the brim of his fedora at Adele and then gave Decklan a warm hug. He pointed out toward the same smoke cloud that gathered over Orcas Island that had recently caught Adele's attention.

"Decklan, did you hear about the accident?"

Decklan appeared to not have any idea what Delroy was referring to. He glanced at Adele and then looked down at Delroy and shook his head.

"No, what accident?"

Delroy's narrow shoulders slumped within the thick blue fabric of his sweatshirt.

"Oh, it's a terrible thing. That little store over in Deer Harbor by your place, it blew up this morning, apparently the result of a propane leak."

All eyes returned to the smoke-filled sky. Adele, shocked by the news, covered her mouth with both her hands. Soon her shock transformed into creeping dread.

"What about Bella Morris?" she asked.

"She's dead," Delroy answerd. "I was just told they pulled her body from the water not more than thirty minutes ago."

Adele felt her legs grow weak and her face go numb. Again, she noted the spot of grime on Decklan's hand, inhaled another breath of fuel-drenched air, and wondered if it was possible a man as effortlessly charming as Decklan Stone could actually be capable of murder.

No, it doesn't make any sense. Why would he hurt Bella?

Adele recalled how angry Decklan was when he found out she had been speaking with others about him.

He very well could have seen me speaking with Bella, too.

"Now what in the hell is *that* all about?" Delroy said.

Both Decklan and Adele followed Delroy's gaze toward the marina's entrance. Three police cruisers with lights flashing had parked in the middle of the entrance and four members of the San Juan County Sheriff's Office were making their way down the dock. The tallest of the four stopped and then pointed directly to where Adele, Decklan and Delroy stood. Delroy readjusted the hat and stared back at the four law enforcement officers.

"It would appear one or all of us are the focus of their attention," he said. "Normally I love to see a man in uniform, but something tells me this isn't going to be one of those times."

As the four armed men drew closer, Adele could see that three were deputies while the oldest, according to his badge, was the county sheriff. It was the sheriff who stopped himself and his men some twenty feet from Delroy's boat and then pointed at Decklan.

"Are you Mr. Decklan Stone?" the sheriff asked.

The hands of the three deputies hovered over their holstered sidearms as they awaited Decklan's answer.

Decklan took a half step forward with his hands at his side. Adele looked up at his face and noted how his expression was a mix of confusion and uncertain curiosity, but he didn't appear fearful.

"Yes, I am," Decklan replied. "Now would you mind telling me what this is about?"

"Mr. Stone, I am Sheriff Leroy Benson."

Decklan gave the fifty-two-year-old sheriff a nod. Benson was a lifelong resident of the islands, a man of average height and build with thinning grey hair and a large bushy mustache that sat watch over a thin-lipped mouth.

"I've heard of you. Now why are you here asking who *I* am, Sheriff Benson?"

Adele sensed the sheriff and his deputies were on edge.

"I'd prefer we discuss this back at the station, Mr. Stone."

Decklan rose to his full height, straightened his shoulders, and casually folded his arms across his chest. He still appeared more curious than fearful over having four armed men standing directly in front of him.

"Are you *asking* me to come with you, or *ordering* me to do so?"

The sheriff's eyes flashed his annoyance.

"I would rather this be done with as little fuss as possible, Mr. Stone."

Adele looked beyond the four law-enforcement officers and saw a small crowd had gathered at the marina entrance. A haughty-faced Tilda Ashland was among them.

Decklan's jaw tightened. He didn't like being told what to do.

"Is this something that requires my attorney to be present?"

Sheriff Benson shifted on his feet as his own hand lowered itself onto the butt of his sidearm.

"At this time, we're just hoping to ask you a few questions."

Decklan gave the sheriff a tight, emotionless smile.

"Then go ahead and ask your questions now, Sheriff, because I would really like to know what this is all about. In fact, I believe it's my right to know."

The sheriff glanced at his men, cleared his throat, and then nodded.

"Okay, Mr. Stone, can you please tell me where you were earlier this morning?"

Decklan's arms remained folded over his chest.

"I was in bed. I was out of bed. I was in the shower. I was having a cup of coffee. I was on my runabout and then over to Sucia…and now I'm here."

The answer clearly made Sheriff Benson more suspicious as his eyes narrowed and he growled the next question.

"Did you hear about the explosion in Deer Harbor, Mr. Stone? The marina store, and the death of Bella Morris?"

Decklan nodded while staring directly into the sheriff's eyes.

"Yes, I did. Just now in fact. What does this have to do with me?"

Sheriff Benson took another step toward Decklan.

"We have a witness placing you at the Deer Harbor store conversing with the deceased less than thirty minutes before the explosion, Mr. Stone. And now *by your own admission*, you fled Deer Harbor by boat shortly after."

Adele watched as Decklan showed the first visible signs of anger toward the law enforcement officers. Not fear, but anger. And then, even more interestingly, sadness. The officers were looking at Decklan as a murderer, and the writer was all too aware of their accusing stares. In their eyes he was a guilty man because he had already been guilty of that very thing for a very long time.

"I never said I fled. And I consider Bella Morris to be a friend, or at the very least, a good person who has always honored my desire for privacy. If you're coming here suggests you think I had anything to do with her death, you are terribly misguided."

The tallest of the three deputies pulled his weapon and proceeded to aim it at Decklan while the sheriff then issued a very clear and concise directive as to what Decklan was to do next.

"Mr. Stone, please place your hands behind your back and turn around."

The other deputies then pointed their weapons at Decklan as well.

"Are you arresting me, Sheriff?"

"What I am doing at this moment, Mr. Stone, is telling you to get your damn hands behind your back—now."

The initially small crowd gathered at the marina entrance had since doubled in size. Many of the people were taking pictures, or videotaping Decklan's worsening situation with the armed officers.

Decklan turned to Delroy Hicks.

"Delroy, I need you to contact Montel Simms in Seattle. He's an attorney. Let him know what's happened."

Delroy's eyes were wide as he nodded his head.

"I'll do it right away," he replied.

Decklan turned his attention to Adele and tried to give her a reassuring smile, though, his eyes betrayed the strain of the moment. They weren't so much the eyes of a guilty man, as those of a man being forced to confront the reality of what so many thought him to be. Namely, that he had murdered his wife, and thus, was likely to have murdered again.

"It would appear I've given you another very interesting chapter to your article, Ms. Plank. I hope you're not offended by my saying I would rather it not be so."

Adele stood silent and unmoving as Decklan was handcuffed and then led toward the marina entrance and the swelling cluster of onlookers. The sheriff walked in front of Decklan and yelled out at the crowd to get back.

The onlookers did as they were told with the exception of Tilda Ashland. She remained very close to the walkway leading away from the marina entrance. She pointed at Decklan as he passed by her and unleashed a raspy cackle of laughter. The display was unnerving enough to the deputies that they hastily swerved to avoid the seemingly unhinged hotel owner.

Delroy shook his head in disgust.

"I do believe that woman has devolved into the most disturbed and unpleasant person I have ever known. Shame on her."

"Do you think he actually had something to do with Bella's death?" Adele asked.

Delroy didn't say anything at first. Then he shrugged.

"At this point, I honestly don't know. It certainly doesn't look good that he chose this morning, of all mornings, to pay me an unannounced visit. And did you notice how dirty his hands were? That is very unlike Decklan."

"Are you going to contact his lawyer?"

Delroy nodded.

"Yes, of course. I said I would. A man is nothing if not a man of his word."

Both Adele and Delroy's gaze returned to the marina entrance where Tilda's shrieking laughter continued to drift across the resort. But for a few others, the crowd had quickly dispersed as life at Roche Harbor returned to whatever version of itself it considered normal. And then even Tilda went silent, abruptly turning and making her way back into her hotel as Phillip followed close behind.

Adele cocked her head as she detected a noise that was both faraway, yet familiar to her. She turned around and saw the faint outline of a small skiff some two hundred yards from the dock heading out toward the channel that was the nautical path back to Deer Harbor from Roche Harbor.

It was Will Speaks.

Delroy looked from Adele to the quickly departing skiff and then back to Adele.

"Do you know that man?"

Adele nodded slowly as she continued to stare at the unmistakably lumpy form that was the son of the former San Juan County sheriff. She was already certain Will's presence in Roche Harbor at the very same moment Decklan Stone was taken into custody in relation to an investigation into the death of Bella Morris by the same county sheriff's office, was no mere coincidence.

And so too was Adele just as certain that two deaths in Deer Harbor, separated by some twenty-seven years, were somehow connected.

"Yes," she answered.

Adele turned and looked at Delroy Hicks who by then already sensed she was about to ask something of him.

"Go on," he said. "What would you like me to do for you?"

"I need to get back onto Orcas Island without anyone knowing, and I need to get there tonight."

Delroy grinned as he placed two fingers onto the brim of his fedora and tipped his hat at the young journalist.

"It would be my pleasure, Ms. Plank. Let's plan to depart here shortly after nightfall. I believe we can simply use the boat Decklan left tied up at the end of the dock. The sheriff doesn't seem too interested in it, which leads me to believe their taking Decklan into custody is bullshit and they know it. If they really thought he had anything to do with what happened this morning in Deer Harbor, they would have secured Decklan's boat as evidence. Or perhaps they're just incompetent. Either way, I could give a damn."

Adele looked down at where Decklan's small runabout sat unused and seemingly waiting to be given a new purpose. It was at that moment a chill ran through her as she realized she would be retracing the same final journey-by-dark-waters from Roche Harbor to Deer Harbor that had resulted in the mysterious death of Calista Stone.

13.

It had been dark for nearly two hours by the time Adele and Delroy quietly made their way to Decklan's runabout. The wind began to pick up late that afternoon, and by evening, the water had turned into a washing machine of churning, white-capped waves.

"I fear this won't be a comfortable ride, Ms. Plank."

Adele pulled her hoodie over her head and nodded.

"I know, but you said taking a larger boat would increase our chances of being spotted by someone, right?"

It was Delroy's turn to nod.

"Yes, that's correct."

"Is it safe?"

Delroy shrugged.

"That's a relative term in these conditions. Will we get there without sinking? Probably. It will be slow going, we're sure to be soaked, but yes, we *should* survive. And you are certain the cove at Decklan's island will provide enough cover to keep the boat hidden from view?"

Adele shivered as a blast of wind pushed her back onto the balls of her feet. The wooden docks groaned as the tips of the tall sailboat masts leaned from one side to the other.

"You've never seen it?"

Delroy reached up to push his hat down to prevent the wind from blowing it off his head.

"No. I've actually only been to Decklan's home twice. Once for his house-warming party when he and Calista first moved in, and a second time shortly after Calista's death. Why are you so intent on going back tonight?"

Adele's jaw clenched as she considered the question.

"I'm not sure. I just feel I've missed something and that maybe Decklan's house is the place to start looking."

Both Adele and Delroy had spoken briefly with Decklan earlier that afternoon. The author's Seattle attorney was out of the country and wouldn't be available until later the following day and the San Juan County Sheriff's Department appeared more than happy to keep Decklan sitting in a jail cell until that time.

Delroy stepped onto the small runabout and then extended a thin and slightly trembling hand to assist Adele in doing the same. Adele wondered if the dying man was in fact up to the journey, especially given the stormy conditions.

"Are you okay to do this, Mr. Hicks? We can wait until the weather gets better."

Delroy scowled and then wagged a bony finger in front of Adele.

"Don't you worry about me. This is the most alive I've felt in years. I'm a bit tired, but I'll be just fine. And I'm sure Decklan keeps a bottle or two of very good wine at the house for us to crack open. Let's just hope nobody from the sheriff's department is already there keeping watch."

The boat's single outboard engine started on the first crank and could barely be heard idling over the sound of the wind. Delroy pointed to the two ropes keeping the craft secured to the dock.

"Go ahead and untie us and let's be on our way," he said.

Adele did as requested, slipping the rope off of the dock cleats and then watching as the runabout drifted slowly away before Delroy put the motor in gear and bumped the idle up so as to allow the craft to begin pushing its way through the nearly two-foot chop that covered the entirety of the marina's watery surface.

Though he didn't say so out loud, Adele sensed Delroy was far more concerned with how much worse the conditions would be once they were in the main channel that separated Roche Harbor from Deer Harbor. He saw three lifejackets poking out from underneath the empty space in the runabout's bow and reached down and grabbed one and then gave it to Adele.

"Put this on, just in case," Delroy shouted.

Though they were just a hundred yards from the dock, the wind's volume had already increased significantly. Adele nodded and then pointed to the other two lifejackets.

"What about you?"

Delroy nodded and then reached down and retrieved a lifejacket for himself as well just as an unusually large wave picked up the front of the runabout and then sent it crashing back down into the next wave's trough as a spray of water washed over the vessel's plastic windshield. By the time Delroy had taken the runabout out of the marina, the waves had increased to nearly three feet and felt to be pummeling the boat from all sides. He pushed the throttle lever forward another half-inch so that they had enough power to break through the waves instead of merely being pushed around by them. Delroy then grabbed Adele and had her sit in the passenger seat directly behind the windshield while he crouched low in the driver's seat hoping enough of the sea spray would be deflected to keep them somewhat dry.

After twenty minutes of struggling against the wind, current, and waves, the runabout entered the San Juan Channel. A darker mass nearly a mile away that served as the backdrop to the nighttime gloom indicated Jones Island was just ahead while looming over Jones Island was the much larger Orcas Island behind it.

Delroy's eyes strained to see to his left and to his right to make certain no other vessels were in the area of his intended path across the channel. With decades of experience navigating these waters, Delroy Hicks knew the distance from his current location to the protected waters of Deer Harbor was just over five miles. He would slowly point the runabout south until he spotted the northern tip of Jones Island and then seek the more protected path that separated Jones Island from the shores of Orcas Island, known as Spring Passage.

Adele gripped the boat's plastic console with both hands as she used her arms as shock absorbers to combat the repeated impact of the bow smashing into yet another wave. The absence of light made the experience that much more frightening. They had agreed to leave the runabout's navigation lights off to ensure as much stealth as possible in case someone was monitoring the boat traffic into and out of Roche and Deer Harbors.

"Shit!" Delroy cried out.

Adele turned to her right and saw him rapidly moving the throttle back and forth and then turning the ignition key on and off.

"What's wrong?" she asked.

At the very same moment Adele spoke those words, an especially large wave hit the side of the runabout with enough force she was pressed against the other side of the hull.

"The motor died! We have no power!"

Adele felt the significance of those words cause her chest to tighten. She knew how much trouble they were suddenly in.

Delroy stood up on unsteady legs and moved to the back of the boat and then turned on the flashlight feature of his cell phone. He bathed the outboard motor in LED light and then shook his head.

"It appears Decklan wasn't lying about his fuel line problem. The same thing just happened to us."

Adele crouched her way to Delroy's side and saw the cause of the stalled motor. The dark grey, high pressure fuel line had broken apart where Decklan had apparently done a temporary duct-tape repair. Delroy was an experienced enough boater to know that the fuel would quickly degrade such tape into a mushy mess, soon rendering the repair useless. He also knew that he should have checked the fuel line prior to leaving Roche Harbor. He silently cursed himself for failing to do so.

The runabout was repeatedly being tossed to the left and right and Adele thought she saw water pooling in an open space directly beneath where the outboard motor was mounted. Delroy noted the concern in her eyes and tried to calm her.

"That's the bilge! It's collecting the water that gets inside the boat, so the water you see there is just what it was designed to do. We're still fine."

Adele gave a stiff nod and tried to appear calm, though, with each wave that lifted the small runabout and then sent it crashing back into the water's surface, she felt her forced façade of calm exterior breaking apart.

"Do you have a pen in your backpack?" Delroy asked.

To Adele it seemed a most unusual question given the circumstances, but she nodded.

Delroy pointed to where the backpack lay next to the passenger seat.

"Good, bring it here."

Adele half stooped and half crawled to her backpack, retrieved the pen, and then made her way to the back of the boat and handed it to Delroy. He took the pen apart until only the hollow, plastic exterior remained. He tried to snap the pen casing in half, but lacked the strength to do so. He sheepishly handed it to Adele and asked her to do it.

With gritted teeth and a loud grunt, she snapped it in two just as another wave broke over the side of the runabout, dumping another half-gallon of water into the hull's interior.

Delroy jammed one end of the broken pen into a damaged section of the fuel line. He strained to push the pen farther into the hard plastic opening. This time Adele didn't wait for him to ask for help. She grasped the pen and jammed it in and then did the same to the other end, securing the fuel line into a continuous section from fuel tank to motor.

"Will it hold?"

Delroy was grinning ear to ear as he shrugged his shoulders.

"Only one way to find out."

He stumbled his way back to the helm and turned the ignition key over. The engine let out a dry cough, belched, shuddered and after a few more seconds, started. Adele peered down at the repair and saw gas seeping out from both ends where the pen casing entered the fuel line. The smell of fuel mixing with the water collecting in the bilge grew stronger.

"It's leaking!"

Delroy motioned for Adele to return to her seat.

"It'll have to work. I guess now would be a good time to quit smoking!"

Adele forced a smile even though she wanted to cry out when the back end of the boat lifted upward and lurched precariously to the side, almost knocking her from the passenger seat.

Delroy put the boat into gear and carefully moved them into the oncoming waves, which by then were cresting higher than three feet. The saltwater smacked into the bow with a snarling, thumping hiss, seemingly determined to push the small runabout over.

Soon, the northern side of Jones Island was no more than a hundred yards away. Adele couldn't quite make out the details of the rocky shoreline, but she could hear the waves crashing into the island's rough, age-pitted skin.

Delroy's recent jovial mood suddenly turned very serious as he found himself unable to make the turn to the right without falling too far into the trough of an oncoming wave and running the risk of having the boat capsize. He also realized that if the motor were to die at that moment, they would likely find themselves dashed upon the rocks of Jones Island.

Adele sensed Delroy's fear which in turn, doubled her own concern. She knew that if an experienced boater like Delroy suddenly appeared to be straining to maintain control of the vessel, the situation had surely entered the realm of a life and death struggle to make it to Deer Harbor alive.

"C'mon, damn it!" Delroy roared as he leaned forward with both his hands tightly gripping the steering wheel. The boat's bow rose up over the crest of a wave, plunged downward, and then repeated the motion. Every third or fourth wave was especially violent, causing the bow to bury itself for a frightening few seconds underneath the water before finally emerging and again climbing up and over the next wave as the motor continued to push the water craft forward.

"Ms. Plank, I need you to hold on very tight. I have to point this thing to the right and when I do, it's going to feel like we're going over. We won't go over though, okay? Do you trust me?"

Adele felt as if she couldn't breathe. She nodded once even as her body began to tremble uncontrollably. Delroy stared into Adele's eyes and gave her a quick grin and then he winked. He began to count down to the moment when the boat would be turned into the deep trough of the next wave.

"One…two…THREE!"

Delroy simultaneously turned and accelerated. Adele could feel the runabout's fiberglass shell shudder violently as it lurched to the right even as a wave struck the boat's side and then pushed it back to the left. Delroy accelerated even more to ensure the bow pointed again to the right. The boat was lifted upward by a wave and then dropped into the trough where it started to roll onto its side.

Adele turned her head and saw swirling night-black waters seemingly inches from her face. She opened her mouth to scream but then abruptly closed it for fear of having it filled with that same water. Then the bow lifted upward again, and Adele was thrown back into her seat and in almost the same instant, tossed to her right as the runabout struggled to remain afloat. A wave crashed over the side and filled the inside with yet more seawater.

Delroy pulled the steering wheel to the left and decelerated to little more than a fast idle as the bow dipped downward and then just as quickly, he accelerated as the boat climbed the crest of the next oncoming wave. Adele watched as Delroy repeated the same slowing down and speeding up maneuver.

They had reached Spring Passage. Orcas Island rose up from the white-capped swells to Adele's left. Delroy pointed to a rocky outcrop some three hundred yards ahead.

"That's Steep Point. Deer Harbor is just around the bend. We're gonna make it."

Adele said nothing. She was still struggling to overcome the fear that gripped her in its unyielding hands. She stared ahead at the inky, sinister hissing liquid that continued to push against the boat. She thought she could hear the water murmur its frustration over its inability to swallow whole the little vessel and its human contents.

It took another half hour before they came within sight of Decklan Stone's private island. It was the longest half-hour of Adele Plank's life. Adele pointed to the area she recalled the partially hidden cove would be found. Both she and Delroy could see the lights of Decklan's house blinking down at them from between the gaps in the tall trees. Delroy cautiously steered the runabout slowly alongside the small island as he strained to find a gap in the rocks that would indicate the partially hidden cove Adele promised was there.

"Ah, that must be it," he said.

Adele finally allowed herself to breathe a sigh of relief as she wiped the seawater from her eyes and face.

Delroy responded by straightening the saltwater-soaked fedora on his head.

"I told you we'd make it. Never a doubt."

As Delroy continued to move the runabout toward the cove's sand and pebble shore, Adele turned around to look back in the direction of the Deer Harbor marina and the burned-out remnants of Bella Morris's store.

We might have made it across that channel, she thought, *but something tells me we're still far from okay.*

14.

"Ah, this is so much better."

Delroy Hicks had made good on his promise to raid Decklan's wine collection and promptly poured himself and Adele glasses from an award-winning Malbec.

They each had blankets wrapped over their still-soaked bodies as they sat in the gloom of the island home's interior. No additional lights were turned on following their arrival as they both agreed doing so might alert law enforcement or someone else that others had entered the Stone residence. Prior to opening the wine, they feasted on hastily made cheese and mustard sandwiches.

"Here's to surviving the storm and the challenge of a good mystery," Adele said.

Adele clinked her glass softly against Delroy's and then took a small sip of the dark red, velvet-textured, wine.

"So, might I ask what you're seeking here, and why it's worth us risking being arrested?"

Adele looked around the great room where she and Delroy sat cross-legged on the wood floor with the open bottle of wine sitting between them. It was then she realized that despite the home's rustic grandeur, it was a place devoid of actual warmth. It felt oddly unlived, almost lifeless, like nothing more than a two-dimensional reflection of the man who resided there.

"He's been very sad for a very long time, hasn't he?"

Delroy took a sip from his own glass and then winced as another series of stabbing pains shot through his abdomen. He waited for the pain to subside before sharing his thoughts.

"Oh, yes, that is undeniable. Decklan Stone is the most miserable creature I have ever known. It is why when we would visit with one another, he always did so by coming to my sailboat and never inviting me here. He wanted to escape this place, the memories of Calista, and the terrible tragedy that was her death. It might be called a cliché by some, but Decklan is truly a man with a broken heart, and it has slowly been killing him just as surely as the waters outside this home killed his beautiful wife all those years ago."

"He told me he tried to leave once."

Delroy appeared genuinely surprised to be told of Decklan's attempt to leave the islands.

"Really? And what happened?"

Adele set her wine on the floor and wrapped the blanket that hung over her shoulders more tightly around her.

"He couldn't do it. He took the runabout in a bad storm just like we did tonight. He made it all the way to Anacortes and then had to turn around and come back here. He said it felt like he was abandoning Calista."

Delroy appeared to be on the verge of tears.

"Calista's death has made Decklan a prisoner, and it appears he's been delivered a life sentence."

Adele nodded. "And now if we assume he had nothing to do with Bella Morris's death, it seems likely someone is trying to set him up. The question that remains though, is *why*?"

Delroy reached out to grab the wine bottle and then proceeded to refill both glasses.

"Indeed. I've been asking myself that very question since we left Roche Harbor, except during those briefly terrifying moments when I thought we might actually die out there."

Adele's eyes widened.

"And?"

Delroy managed to combine a simultaneous drink of wine and a shrug of his shoulders.

"And nothing. I have no idea who would wish to do such a thing."

"Well, *someone* had to have informed the sheriff they saw Decklan speaking to Bella shortly before the explosion."

Delroy began to nod his head slowly when suddenly he sat up straight, which in turn caused the blanket to fall away and collapse onto the floor behind him.

"The sheriff."

Adele scowled.

"Yeah, someone spoke with the sheriff. The question is who?"

Delroy snapped his fingers together.

"Exactly. The sheriff spoke with the sheriff. I mean to say, the *former* sheriff, Sheriff Speaks was the one who informed the current sheriff that he saw Decklan talking with Bella. Sheriff Speaks lives here on Orcas Island, correct? He also keeps a boat in the marina, yes?"

Adele was nodding her head as her mind raced to put together the pieces of the puzzle Delroy was laying out for her.

"You're right."

Delroy continued to speak as his own excitement caused the volume of his words to increase.

"And the current sheriff, Sheriff Benson, he worked for Sheriff Speaks. He owes his *entire career* to Speaks. Benson was who Speaks personally endorsed to replace him."

"So, you're saying we can't trust Sheriff Benson?"

Delroy simultaneously grunted and flinched, gestures which made clear the idea of trusting Sheriff Benson to be inconceivable to him.

"Hell no, we can't trust him. Not if this thing, whatever it is, somehow involves Sheriff Speaks. If there are any skeletons in Sheriff Benson's past, you can bet Speaks knows of them and that knowledge gives him leverage. It gives him power. Men like Martin Speaks rarely give up such power. And if he *is* involved, and therefore had something to do with Bella's death, then we best realize we are dealing with a man capable of killing a human being in order to keep secret whatever thing it is he's hiding."

That declaration caused both Adele and Delroy to go silent as they both realized the gravity of the situation they suddenly found themselves involved in.

"I think whoever was standing outside this house when I first came to interview Decklan followed me to Bellingham," Adele said. "It was a man. He was in the library basement with me when I was doing research for the interview. I didn't want to think about it much since it happened, but now I have to wonder if he was there not just to scare me. That maybe he was there to hurt me, or possibly worse."

Delroy's chin fell against his narrow, bony chest as he peered up at Adele from underneath the brim of his fedora.

"You know, I've spent most of my adult life thinking guns are horrible and dangerous things, but I wish we had one with us now."

Adele lifted her glass and nodded.

"I couldn't agree more."

Her wine glass was nearly empty when Adele leaned her head to the side. Delroy noticed the gesture.

"What is it?"

Adele held a finger up to her lips.

"Ssshhh, I think I hear someone coming."

It was the sound of an outboard motor, and Adele was certain it was getting closer. Delroy began to nod his head.

"Yes, I hear it now too. The storm's died down, hardly any wind outside. I do believe it's coming this way. Maybe it's someone from the sheriff's department.

Adele felt the same familiar fear rise up within her as she had experienced in the basement of the university library. There was no rational explanation for why she felt the same. Rather, she simply knew it to be. Whoever was on the boat outside wasn't law enforcement but rather the same man who had come for her in Bellingham.

"We need to hide," she whispered.

Delroy lifted himself off the floor with a grimace and began to pick up his blanket and then paused.

"What if it's Decklan?"

Adele silently considered the possibility.

Maybe it was Decklan who followed me to Bellingham.

Though it was certainly possible, Adele's instincts informed her it wasn't likely to be Decklan stepping onto the private island in the middle of the night.

The sound of the boat motor suddenly died.

Adele pointed to the staircase.

"Upstairs, hurry!"

The two grabbed their blankets, glasses, Adele's ever-present backpack, the nearly empty bottle of wine, and then made their way up to the second-level hallway. Adele motioned for Delroy to follow her into the same guestroom she had stayed in earlier. Once inside, she proceeded to close the door until just a sliver of an opening remained that allowed a partial view out into the hallway.

"Now stay still," she said.

Delroy slowly placed the glasses and bottle onto one of the two bedside tables and then walked gingerly to where Adele stood on the opposite side of the room looking through the window into the inky darkness that was beyond the other side of the glass.

Both Adele and Delroy heard whistling coming from outside, which confirmed to each of them they were no longer the only ones on the small island. Delroy took a sharp inward breath as the sound of someone trying to open the locked front door echoed throughout the home.

Seconds later he felt Adele's hand shoving him away from the window. She let him know what she saw with a whispered hiss.

"He's right below us. I think he's trying the back entrance."

They heard the unmistakable creak of a door opening. Someone else was in the home.

Heavy, shuffling footsteps echoed below them from the kitchen. Adele tiptoed to the cracked bedroom door and put her eye up to the small gap that allowed her to partially see down the hallway toward the top of the staircase.

Whoever had entered was still in the kitchen. Adele heard shuffling, drawers opening, and then a mechanical clicking noise. She nearly screamed when the sound of a woman speaking erupted from the first floor.

It was the voice of Bella Morris.

"Hello, Mr. Stone, this is your neighbor Bella Morris over here in Deer Harbor. I was hoping to speak with you about something I heard late yesterday, something I think you should know. I'd feel better telling you in person. You might think I'm crazy, and perhaps you'd be right, but I really need to tell you what I heard. Maybe it's nothing and maybe it's something, but I'd feel better at least letting you know. Please call me back at the store or you can stop by in person if you like. Good-bye."

Adele looked behind her and saw Delroy staring with his mouth hanging open. He had heard the message as well. Then a voice cried out from the kitchen.

"Stupid old bitch. Mind your own d-d-damn business. That's what my mother would say. She taught me that. But you won't say anything. No, you won't. Not anymore."

Delroy stood shoulder to shoulder with Adele as they collectively held their breath and listened to the shouting voice.

"Not anymore! Not anymore! Not anymore!"

Delroy gasped as his hand went to his side. He took a step back and bumped the nightstand. The wine bottle tipped over and rolled onto the floor with a muffled clunk-thud.

The shouting below went silent.

Adele closed her eyes tightly and waited.

Please don't come up here.

A footstep struck the bottom stair, followed by a second, and then a third.

It's the damn library basement all over again, she thought.

Delroy whispered an apology for having knocked over the wine bottle.

"I'm so sorry. I'm just a clumsy old fool."

Adele reached down slowly and picked up the bottle by its thick glass neck. If the man coming up the stairs intended to make his way into the bedroom, she had no intention of allowing herself to be an easy victim.

A loud, shrill whistle pierced the nighttime silence outside Decklan's home. Adele let out a long, grateful sigh as she heard footsteps return to the kitchen and then the home's back door open and close. She returned as quickly and quietly as possible to her earlier location near the bedroom window and looked out to see the same burning cigarette light she had seen the last time she stayed overnight as Decklan's guest.

Two male voices murmured outside, but their tones remained too low for Adele to hear what was being said. The men abruptly left the area below the window, and a short time later, the sound of an outboard motor coming to life was heard, followed by the motor's increasingly distant drone as the boat took off across the nighttime waters on its way back to Deer Harbor.

"There were two of them?" Delroy asked.

Adele nodded.

"Yes, and I'm almost certain who they were."

Without saying more, Adele moved out into the hallway and then down the stairs, going slowly at first, and then after making certain no-one else was in the home, she moved into the kitchen and located the answering machine.

The tape was gone.

Delroy lightly hit the countertop with a closed fist.

"Damn! They took the tape with them."

Adele's face broke out into a sly grin as she reached into her back pocket and withdrew her old recorder. She proceeded to replay Bella's message, having earlier kept her wits enough to record it as it was first being played by the intruder.

Delroy looked at her with bemused amazement and an entirely new level of respect.

"Why you clever, clever girl..."

15.

"You intend to make a call? I don't believe we have service out here."

Adele shook her head at Delroy as her finger moved from left to right across her cell phone screen.

"No, I took a picture of a photo originally taken years ago in Roche Harbor. I think I might have missed something. Here it is."

Delroy stood in the kitchen's near-absolute darkness and watched Adele's eyes peering at the illuminated image on her phone. She hit the zoom feature, stared at it a second longer, and then nodded her head.

"Look at the person in the background behind Decklan and Calista. Do you recognize him?"

Delroy squinted as he held Adele's phone in front of him."

"You mean the young man there?"

The former professor's head snapped up as his eyes widened.

"That's Will Speaks—the sheriff's son."

Adele abruptly turned and began to leave the kitchen. She paused and pointed back at Delroy.

"Wait here. I'll be right back."

Delroy could hear Adele running up the steps to the second floor and then seconds later, running back down them. She entered the kitchen with her backpack and proceeded to retrieve the French magazine she had taken from the library that contained the long-ago feature story on Decklan and Calista Stone.

She scanned the photographs in the article using the magnifier app on her cell phone. After a few seconds she tapped one of the magazine's black-and-white pictures with her finger.

"There, take a look."

Delroy gazed at the photo showing Decklan and Calista walking hand in hand toward the entrance to the Roche Harbor Hotel. Adele handed him her cell phone.

"Now look at it with this. Check out the upper right-hand corner of the photo."

Delroy leaned down until his face was just inches from the magazine. Then he stood up and shook his head.

"It's the Speaks boy again, staring at them."

"Two photographs," Adele said, "taken weeks, or perhaps even months apart, and Will Speaks happens to be in both of them. Why is that?"

Delroy returned Adele's phone and stuffed his hands into his front pockets.

"It does appear to be an oddly remarkable coincidence."

"No, not if Will Speaks was watching them, *following* them."

Delroy removed his hat and ran his fingers through his hair.

"Why on earth would he be doing that? I understand he suffered some mental challenges in his youth, likely exacerbated by his mother's death, but now that he's a man one would hardly know that to be the case. He seems normal enough, at least what little I've seen of him."

Adele recalled how Will had looked at her in Deer Harbor after her visit with Decklan Stone. She also remembered something Will's father told him that same morning, poking his son as he did so.

Don't you even think about it, the former sheriff had said.

Adele had no idea what those words meant, but believed she was getting closer to something very significant. The former sheriff had been adamant she not return to Decklan's island home before Bella Morris intervened on Adele's behalf, shooing the sheriff away.

And now Bella is dead, but not before trying to speak with Decklan about something important.

Adele lookcd at Dclroy.

"Consider the fact that whoever broke into Decklan's home knew he had one of those old-fashioned answering machines. Hardly anybody uses those things anymore, but those two men outside this house knew. The one who came inside went right for it. You said yourself Decklan didn't even have you over here. He would visit you in Roche Harbor. So, knowing that, who might have known about the answering machine? Maybe Bella mentioned having left a message on an answering machine, but then who would have had the opportunity to hear her say that?"

Delroy's eyes narrowed. He sensed Adele was closing in on something he feared might be better left alone.

"You have some kind of plan working itself out in that young head of yours, don't you?"

As crazy and dangerous as it might prove to be, Adele was determined to see it through. When she told Delroy of her intent, he chuckled and then nodded his agreement, though, he was clearly nervous. He would help her because, in doing so, he thought it possible to help his friend Decklan. Delroy feared the writer was losing his will to live, and he had no intention of outliving Decklan Stone.

The two slept in shifts, worried the visitors might return to the island. They managed just a few hours between them.

Delroy knocked lightly on Adele's bedroom door and cleared his throat.

"Are you sure you still want to do this thing?"

Adele needed no time to answer. Her resolve persisted.

"Yes."

Delroy appeared to be working the kinks out of his neck as he rolled his head from side to side. Then he gave Adele a long look, shrugged his shoulders, and confirmed his own willingness to help her with the plan.

"Okay, then let's go."

The walk the two made to the hidden cove and the awaiting runabout brought about the benefit of a water-chilled, pre-morning breeze that pushed back any residual fatigue, which in turn sharpened their senses and further solidified Adele's determination to proceed.

The trip across the water to Deer Harbor went smoothly, benefitted greatly by the absence of any waves. Delroy moved the small boat to the very back corner of the marina where it was least likely to be seen. He and Adele tied it up to the dock and then began to make their way toward the ramp that connected the marina to the island.

The stench of burned wood and plastic permeated the area, growing more intense the closer they came to what remained of Bella's store. Delroy paused at the blackened wood frame. It had yellow and black police tape wrapped around it that read, "Do Not Cross."

"What a terrible shame," he said. "This was a fixture of the islands, as was Bella herself."

Adele ignored Delroy's maudlin sentiment. She had a more immediate concern as she pointed at something.

"There it is. That's his boat."

Delroy could see the outline of a small, battered fishing boat.

"I do hope you're sure, because I don't want to be involved in potentially sinking the wrong one."

Adele nodded.

"Yes, that's it. That's the one."

Delroy glanced at the vessel and then looked back at Adele. He let out a quick sigh and then made his way down to the boat.

"Keep an eye out for anyone. I'm going aboard to find a wrench."

Adele stood at the top of the ramp as a lookout. She estimated they had no more than fifteen or twenty minutes before daylight.

"Found one. He's got tools scattered all over this thing. He appears to have the organizational habits of a homeless man."

Delroy emerged from the back of the fishing boat holding a small wrench. He swung his legs over and onto the narrow, metal-framed swim step that hung off the very back of the vessel as Adele silently prayed the old man didn't fall off into the water with a loud splash that might alert others to their presence.

"This won't be fun," he grumbled.

Delroy groaned as he leaned down onto all fours and then slipped his thin right arm through the narrow gap between the boat's swim step frame and the aluminum transom. He sucked in a breath between clenched teeth when the frigid water encased the entirety of his forearm as his fingers ran along the water-slimed exterior of the transom.

He had been the one to suggest using the sheriff's boat as a distraction but as his teeth began to chatter from the water's seemingly near freezing temperature, Delroy began to regret the idea.

Then he located the small brass drain plug and allowed himself a satisfied grin.

There you are you little bastard!

Delroy reached down through the swim step gap with his left hand and then passed the wrench into his right hand, his lower body nearly sliding off into the water in the process.

Easy, old boy. You got a job to do, now just get it done.

The plug wouldn't budge. He tried again, and then again, failing each time to break the drain plug free.

Delroy's frustration grew quickly. He forgot about the cold water, forgot about slipping off the swim step, and even forgot about the risk of someone seeing him on a boat that wasn't his. His lips pulled back into a wolflike snarl as he yanked the wrench with every bit of strength left in his cancer-weakened body.

The drain plug moved.

After a few more tugs, Delroy was able to use his hand to unscrew the plug from the hull, but realized too late the cold temperatures had rendered his fingers slow to respond and the plug fell from his grasp and drifted downward toward the marina's mud and eel-grass bottom some ten feet below.

As Delroy stood up with a hushed grunt, he could hear water trickling into the boat's bilge. He tossed the wrench into the boat and then carefully stepped back onto the dock while also trying to catch his breath. His fedora sat where he had left it atop one of the white electrical boxes the boats in the marina used to plug into shore power. Soon the hat was back on Delroy's head as he made his way up the ramp toward Adele.

"Are we good?" Adele asked.

Delroy grinned.

"Indeed, we are. There's a good deal of water coming into the boat. Before long, the bilge pump will kick on, and that'll get the attention of someone around here. Then they'll make a quick call to the sheriff that he's got a serious problem. My guess is he'll be down here within the hour."

Adele scanned the area for any sign of someone else being nearby but found none.

"Okay, until then we hide and wait."

Delroy pointed to a nook across the main road that was partially hidden by a tall evergreen tree growing out of the hillside between two large homes that had sweeping views of the marina and island waters beyond.

"Up there would work. We can see everyone coming and going and still have most of the marina in our sightline as well."

Adele agreed and the two made their way up to the road. By the time they reached it, the last of the nighttime darkness had almost completely dissipated. From somewhere on the other side of Deer Harbor, perhaps near Decklan's island, came the long and lonely wail of a single loon that carried across the glasslike waters and rose up to echo over the broad-branched shoulders of the trees that stretched out above the island's shores.

It was a sound both beautiful and ominous that shot a brief, cold quiver up and down Adele's spine.

"Fortune smiles upon us," Delroy said. "The Native American tribes of this region have long considered that song to be a harbinger of harmony and truth."

Adele glanced at him with uncertainty.

"Really?"

"Indeed. Do you know the loon, unlike most other birds, has *solid* bones? It is what allows them to dive so far beneath the surface of the water and find the truth that hides beneath."

The loon's call sounded again, just as the light of the morning sun broke out over the hillside and caressed the Deer Harbor waters below.

Adele nudged Delroy with her elbow.

"I sure hope you're right about that bird out there. We could use some harmony and truth."

Delroy rested his chin on the arms that he had folded over his knees and smiled, an act which deepened the already crevice-like lines that mapped either side of his mouth and the corners of his eyes.

"As do I, young lady. As do I."

Within ten minutes, an older, tall, balding and heavily bearded man lumbered down the middle of the road with his long arms swinging at his sides. He turned onto the path leading to the marina.

Delroy leaned toward Adele.

"That's Old Jack. I haven't seen him in nearly ten years. He works on a lot of boats around here. Really knows his stuff. He's something of a local legend among all of the area boat owners."

Adele remembered that Martin Speaks mentioned that it was Old Jack who kept Decklan's Chris Craft in such good condition.

"I think you best get yourself ready," Delroy whispered. "If anyone were to notice something taking on water, it would be Old Jack."

Delroy's prediction proved accurate. Mere minutes later they heard Old Jack speaking loudly into his cell phone at the top of the marina ramp.

"You might want to get yourself down here quick, Sheriff. I can hear the water coming in. Your bilge pump is working overtime trying to keep up. We might need to pull her out of the water pronto or you'll be pulling her off the bottom before too long."

It was Adele's turn to whisper to Delroy.

"Well done, Professor. This is going about as smoothly as we could have hoped for."

Soon a rust-speckled pickup truck pulled up to the marina entrance and both Martin and Will Speaks stepped out and quickly made their way down the ramp to their boat. Adele and Delroy could hear the former sheriff cursing loudly at the water coming into it.

"Okay, I'm calling the taxi to take me to the sheriff's home. You stay here and then message me if they leave before I get back."

Delroy tipped his fedora, underneath which his eyes glimmered with excitement. He was truly enjoying playing the part of Adele's accomplice in the mysterious adventure he found himself involved in.

"Be careful, young lady, and please call me at the first sign of any trouble."

Delroy watched as Adele jogged down the road until she was out of sight of the marina. She spoke into her cell phone and then waited for the cab to arrive. When it did, she opened the back door and then paused to give Delroy a quick wave. He waved back and then heard a subconscious whisper of warning that he should try and stop her from going to the former sheriff's isolated home without him but by the time Delroy pushed himself up onto his feet, Adele was already gone. The soft, distant drone of the departing taxi's tires against the pavement was the only sign she had been there at all.

Adele was going into a potentially dangerous unknown and doing so entirely on her own.

16.

"You mind me asking how you know the sheriff?"

Adele sat in the back of Joe's taxi quietly building up the courage to actually break into the home of a former law enforcement officer.

"I'm a reporter," she replied. "It's for an article."

Adele could see Joe glancing at her in the rearview mirror. His eyes briefly lingered on her and then he shrugged, an indication he no longer cared what her intentions might be.

"Don't think I've ever dropped anyone off at his house is all. I figure Sheriff's never been one for entertaining people. Truth be told, I think the guy is just a puffed up, self-important, old prick. His boy seems all right. A bit off in the head, but nice enough. He sure likes being on the water. I see him out there all the time on that little skiff of his. Rain or shine, it doesn't matter. Can't say I blame him. Means he doesn't have to listen to his old man's bitching. I remember him bragging to me a few summers back about how he was taking it all the way to Bellingham and back on a single tank of gas. That's quite a trip in such a little boat, but like I said, he's always been a little off."

Adele didn't respond. She was so focused on sticking to her plan that she hardly heard the taxi driver's words at all. Only when the car came to a stop on the side of a narrow, heavily treed road did she look up and realize they had arrived at the destination that was the gated drive to the home of Martin and Will Speaks.

"You need me to wait here for you?" Joe asked. "I don't mind."

Adele was grateful for the offer, realizing Joe could add another layer of security for her in case Martin or Will returned.

"Actually, yes, that would be great. Thank you so much."

Joe shrugged again and then picked up a book from the front passenger seat.

"It's no problem. Give me a chance to get some reading done. I figure it's about time I read this thing since the guy who wrote it lives around here."

Adele saw the book's cover and realized it was a copy of *Manitoba*.

Joe held the book up.

"You read it?"

Adele nodded.

"Yeah."

Minutes later she was adjusting her backpack and walking toward the Speaks home. A row of aged pine trees bordered either side of the long drive, their branches reaching out over her head and creating swathes of shadow that made Adele quicken her pace.

It was nearly a half mile before she came upon a large, two-story farmhouse that rose up from a large clearing. The tall grass appeared not to have been cut in years. In some spots it was well over three feet. The home itself leaned drunkenly to its side, and its dull, white exterior was badly chipped and faded. One of the windows was boarded over with a section of water-stained plywood.

Large sections of the roof were covered in blue tarp and kept in place by concrete cinder blocks. The rotted steps leading to the covered front porch had several large gaps where it appeared a foot had broken through.

If Adele didn't know better, she would have thought the house had been abandoned long ago. Rusted remnants of various vehicles dotted the landscape around the residence. A large, reddish barn missing its roof stood some three hundred yards to the right of the home, its entrance almost fully concealed by the tall grass.

The area was oddly absent of any noise. Even the wind seemed determined to avoid the place. Adele was shocked that human beings could live in such conditions. She moved carefully up the porch steps and stood just outside the front door. Her right hand trembled as it reached out to grasp the door's handle.

Locked, she thought. *Did you think it would be that easy?*

Adele strode through the tall grass toward the rear of the home. She reached another porch where a piece of plywood attached to hinges served as a makeshift backdoor. There were also three old plastic lawn chairs facing the back portion of the multi-acre property. A coffee can overflowing with cigarette butts rested between two of the chairs. The stench of the stale tobacco was almost overwhelming, but then Adele realized the smell was actually coming from inside the home.

She stepped carefully onto the porch and pulled the door open. Adele took a long, slow breath and was about to enter the home when she stopped and turned around.

Three chairs.

She looked at each of the chairs more closely. Two of the seats had deep indentations.

Martin and Will Speaks.

There was barely any indentation on the bottom of the third chair, indicating it was hardly used, or used by someone not heavy enough to make one.

Adele could feel her heart pounding inside her chest. A layer of sweat covered her face. The pieces of a puzzle she didn't want to imagine to actually be real were actually falling into place.

She knew what must be done.

The answer, however horrible it might prove to be, was to be found within the home.

Adele walked inside.

She reached up to cover her nose and mouth, fighting the urge to vomit as her senses were assaulted by the stench of rotting food, nicotine, and human waste. The floor below her feet was covered in refuse, a combination of garbage, dirt, and cigarette ash. Flies buzzed over the dishes and scum-water that filled the sink.

An old, nicotine-yellowed fridge hummed quietly in the corner of the kitchen. Next to it was a little eating table covered in stacks of newspapers and food-encrusted forks and knives. Three chairs surrounded the table.

Yet more dirty dishes were piled atop a black stove stained with the remnants of meals from days, weeks, and months past. Adele's eyes adjusted to the low light of the kitchen interior as she looked down a narrow hallway that led from the kitchen into the home's main lower level.

The short walk down that hallway revealed walls scattered with fist-sized holes along with empty picture frames. Adele emerged from the hallway into the living room and found it surprisingly clean and free of clutter. Even the dark brown and orange shag carpet that covered the floor appeared to have been regularly vacuumed. A dark, red-cloth couch ran nearly the entire length of the back wall in front of which was a simple black coffee table. On the opposite wall from the couch was an old television with a pair of rabbit ears on top of it. The TV didn't appear to be plugged in. The entire room seemed to be an attempt by the home's residents to represent a point in time from which they didn't wish to move beyond, a kind of remembrance of what once was.

Even the cream-colored walls looked to have been kept almost free from the yellow nicotine stains that covered every other corner of the house.

Adele turned toward the narrow, wood-framed staircase that led upstairs, but found it in such disrepair she feared it might be incapable of supporting her weight. The third step was missing entirely and opened up into a pitch-black space beneath the stairs out of which Adele thought she smelled something even more wretched than the rotting stench from the kitchen.

Beyond the staircase was another narrow hall that included three doors. The first door opened into the home's only bathroom. It was in a similar state as the kitchen with the added attraction of being covered in a thick layer of urine and human waste both on the floor and the walls nearest the toilet. The single sink was badly cracked, and the wood countertop was nearly rotted entirely from years of water seeping through the broken sink. Adele reached down and opened the small cabinet door under the sink and screamed before slamming the door shut. She backed out of the bathroom while trying hard to calm herself.

Underneath the sink was a nest that included a cluster of newborn rodents that shrieked hungrily at the sound of the cabinet door being opened. Just before slamming the door shut, Adele was certain she saw a dark blur leap into a hole in the wall behind the sink and knew it to be an especially large, full-grown rat.

With her legs still weak and shaking from the critter scare, Adele made her way down the hallway to the first of the two remaining doors and found it already open. Inside was a small bedroom with a badly stained mattress on the floor, accompanied by piles of dirty clothes and empty pop cans. The walls were papered with a pattern of sunflowers and on the wall behind the mattress were the painted words, "Will's Room."

Adele moved quickly to the second room across the hall from the first. The door was closed and would only open after she gave it a hard shove with her shoulder. The door's hinges groaned loudly to reveal a space similar in size to the first bedroom, but with more furnishings.

A double-sized oak bed frame was in the corner with a window overlooking the backyard area. A single, dark-blue blanket was neatly laid out over the mattress, accompanied by two pillows encased in matching blue coverings. The smell of cigarettes was strongest in this room, and a large ashtray on the nightstand next to the bed overflowed with spent cigarettes and ash.

On the other side of the room was a small walk-in closet without a door. The space had just a few olive-colored work shirts hanging from a single bar, along with a neatly pressed San Juan County Sheriff's uniform, and a pair of brightly polished black dress shoes.

A large freezer that appeared to be unplugged sat against another of the room's walls. Why Martin Speaks would keep an unused freezer in his bedroom made no sense, but then again almost nothing in the house made sense.

Two sets of shoes sat at the end of the bed. The first was a worn-out pair of black rubber boots. The second was a smaller pair of old canvas boating shoes. Adele stood staring at them, trying to remember where she had seen them before.

Her eyes widened. She quickly removed her backpack, placed it on the bed, and then withdrew the old article on Calista Stone's death. She found the photograph of Sheriff Martin Speaks with the caption that read:

Sheriff Speaks holding the only thing found following the search for Calista Stone, a shoe that her husband later identified as belonging to his wife.

Adele looked from the photo to the pair of shoes at the end of the bed.

It's the same shoe, she thought. *Except there's the other one, too. If only the one shoe was found floating in the water, why are both shoes in this house twenty-seven years later?*

Adele reached down and picked up the shoe that was being held by Martin Speaks in the newspaper article so that she could confirm it was in fact the same one. In the photograph, a portion of the rubber toe appeared to have a darkened gouge in it. Adele stared at the shoe in her hands and located the exact same mark on the toe.

From somewhere outside, the far-off sound of a motor caused Adele to panic and drop the shoe onto the wood floor, where it hit with a thump. She ran down the hall into the living room to look through a window fully expecting to see Martin and Will Speaks returning in their pick-up truck. Instead, she realized the noise was the sound of a small, single-engine plane flying overhead, likely on its way to the Friday Harbor Airport.

It was then Adele realized she had left her backpack in the bedroom. She went back into the room and hastily returned the shoe to its place at the end of the bed and then swung the backpack over her shoulders.

I need to take pictures before I leave.

Adele took out her phone and began photographing the home's interior. She took shots of both bedrooms, the living room, and the kitchen. She avoided the bathroom, still too frightened by the things living under the sink. Once back outside, she sent Delroy a text.

Almost finished here. All clear?

After an excruciating minute of waiting, she finally received a reply.

They are still at the boat but could be leaving soon. Good if you get out of there. Find anything?

Adele made certain the backdoor was fully closed.

Maybe. Will talk soon. On my way.

Adele was soon ducking under the locked gate and crossing the road toward Joe's awaiting taxi.

"How'd it go?" he asked.

Adele shrugged while scanning through the pictures she had taken.

"It went fine. Take me back to Deer Harbor, please."

They were nearly halfway to the marina when Adele suddenly cried out.

"Turn around! I have to go back!"

When Joe glanced into the rearview mirror with a look of confusion and continued to drive toward Deer Harbor, Adele slammed the back of the driver's seat with her hand.

"Turn around! Right now! And hurry as fast as you can!"

Joe shook his head, hit the brakes, made a sharp U-turn, and then pushed down on the accelerator while wondering why his passenger was suddenly so panicked.

Adele's eyes never left the image on her phone. She cursed herself for having missed it while standing in the room.

It was right there in front of me.
The truth still waited to be discovered in the derelict home—a truth that would finally at long last be known.

17.

At the very moment Adele Plank screamed for Joe to turn his taxi around, Decklan Stone was preparing to kill himself.

Just ten minutes earlier he had been dropped off at his private dock by two deputies. Upon his arrival there, he discovered someone had taken his runabout from Roche Harbor. Decklan didn't care who might have done so. In the time between his being taken into custody and his release, he had stopped caring about anything. He watched the aluminum law enforcement vessel back away from his island and then abruptly turn in the water and speed away. None of the boat's occupants bothered to look back at him as he held up his hand to wave goodbye.

He knew why.

For the last twenty-seven years he had *always* known why.

Since Calista's death, Decklan Stone was a monster in the eyes of those who chose to condemn him for his wife's passing. And though he had effectively retreated from their world, he could not retreat from his own sense of guilt and soul-crushing loss, leading him to always wonder if they were, in fact, right about him.

Perhaps he was a monster after all.

The man known by others simply as "the writer" had finally reached his limit. Convinced he had long ago lived beyond his expiration date, Decklan only wanted twenty-seven years of accumulated looks and whispered accusations to end, and to allow the world, once and for all, to move on without him.

It's the humane thing to do…

People had long disappointed Decklan but there was no greater disappointment than that which he felt for himself. He recalled looking up and seeing the disgust in Tilda's eyes as he was marched by her with his hands cuffed behind him. He saw his image reflected in those same eyes, saw how small and inconsequential he had become. She wished him dead. He saw too the others who pointed at him, likely whispering he was the writer who had killed his wife.

Why not just give Tilda and everyone else what they so clearly want?

As he sat unmoving and silent in his jail cell, Decklan began to entertain the possibility of ending it all. The more he considered it, the greater its appeal became.

He was just so tired—so very, very tired.

By the time his Seattle attorney arrived to expedite his release from the holding cell, Decklan had made up his mind. Thinking his life held so little remaining purpose, he had no intention of seeing another day to its conclusion.

Years earlier he had made certain that upon his death, his island residence would be given over to a local animal shelter. He thought it appropriate that something nature had made so beautiful should be used by the creatures that inhabited the San Juan Islands.

He felt a brief pang of guilt when he considered what his death might do to his one remaining friend, Delroy Hicks, but he knew that Delroy was just as likely to follow him in death soon enough.

That left Adele Plank.

Decklan had come to care for and admire the young college journalist. She had shown him the kind of consideration and respect that had been missing for so much of his adult life. But he had granted her the initial interview, and his death would only expedite the genesis of her career. The thought gave Decklan some comfort that he was still capable of helping someone.

Once the county law enforcement vessel had vanished from view, Decklan turned to stare at the Chris Craft. The vessel appeared to stare back at him, whispering for Decklan to step aboard and revisit an old friend.

Soon he was seated at the upper helm and backing the forty-foot cruiser away from his island home for the final time. The moment he heard the low-pitched, gurgling growl of the twin inboard gas engines, the writer knew he was making the right choice. He thought it only appropriate that his final moments would be upon the very same vessel that he and Calista had loved so much until it became the source for both the tragedy of Calista's death, and the prolonged tragedy that was the remainder of Decklan Stone's life.

Decklan looked up to see the brilliant, white-feathered head of a bald eagle staring down at him as the great bird of prey flew over the Chris Craft. The sky was bathed in soft blue hues, and the wind had a touch of warmth upon it, an undeniable hint of the summer soon to be. Calista had loved the island summers so much.

As Decklan idled the boat past the front portion of his island, he glanced behind him and saw the two chairs jutting out from the cliff that overlooked the water below. He wondered if there was in fact something beyond the painfully brief and tumultuous lives that most people were forced to live. Would some version of an afterlife afford him the chance to sit with Calista in those chairs once again?

That possibility made Decklan grin as he guided the Chris Craft into deeper waters. He would know soon enough.

He took the first drink from the whiskey bottle after arriving at the approximate center of Deer Harbor. It was nearly three hundred yards in any direction to the shore. The Chris Craft's engines were shut off and its anchor let out to hold the vessel's position. Within five minutes, half the bottle was emptied.

Decklan had always considered the area to be the place where Calista had likely fallen off the boat and into the water. He had long been haunted by images of her crying out for him as she watched the Chris Craft continue on its way toward their home. It wouldn't have been very long before she realized what was going to happen. The frigid water would rob her of the ability to move, to stay afloat, and thus, to stay alive. Perhaps if Decklan had pushed aside his own stubborn pride and checked on her inside of the boat, he would have had time to locate and save her. He didn't do that, though.

I left her to die out here, all alone...just like the kittens.

Decklan could feel his head swimming in the numbing pool of his emerging drunkenness. He took yet another drink, and then another, until finally the whiskey bottle's contents were spent. His stomach attempted a revolt, wanting to expel the alcohol, but Decklan clamped his jaws shut and waited for the threatened nausea to pass.

He scanned the surroundings, noting Orcas Island and San Juan Island, as well as the southern tip of Jones Island. Decklan had to squint and concentrate in order to focus the view. He could hear the waves crashing against the collective island shores in the distance. It was a sound that had always brought him comfort, even in the darkest days immediately following his wife's passing.

Decklan was grateful to have that same sound with him at the time of his own chosen conclusion.

He stood up on legs wobbly with drink and had to reach out to prevent himself from falling over. The alcohol had served its intended purpose in debilitating him beyond recovery. Decklan moved to the side of the boat and shuffled slowly toward the bow and then flung his legs over the stainless-steel railing so that the only thing preventing him from falling over into the dark and swirling waters below were his hands grasping that same railing behind him.

Another gust of warm wind brushed against his face, like the cautious caress of a gentle lover. Decklan imagined it to be the hand of Calista telling him that what he was doing was right.

That it was time.

Warm-wet tears streamed down his face as his hands lightened their grip on the railing. He could feel the weight of his body wanting to fall forward.

I'm so sorry, Calista. I loved you so much. I wasn't a perfect man, but I was a man who loved you in every way I knew how. I've been little more than a shadow of a shadow since you were taken from me. My life has no life left. I can't pretend to care about wanting to see another day. Please forgive me—for everything.

Decklan opened his eyes for the last time. He would enter the water, allow himself to sink well below the surface, open his mouth, and then take a deep breath and fill his lungs. Being unable to experience the last twenty-seven years of his life with Calista, Decklan was now determined to die alone just as his wife had.

It's what I deserve.

He counted down from three and then found himself unable to let go of the railing. He was disgusted by his cowardice.

Damn you, God! Let me have just this one thing! Allow me this choice!

Again, Decklan counted down, this time speaking the numbers out loud.

"Three . . . two . . . one."

Decklan's hands still refused to let go. He lifted his head upward and his mouth opened wide. He wanted to scream, but the only sound that came was a softly pleading moan, the embodiment of twenty-seven years of repressed pain, rage, and regret.

Decklan heard the sound of a motor coming from the direction of Deer Harbor and knew he must act soon before someone realized what he intended to do. His chin fell against his chest and one of his hands finally relinquished the railing, causing his body to lurch sideways.

With his eyes closed tight, Decklan's mind tried to recall an image of Calista but instead it was Tilda Ashland's snarling, accusatory glare that stared back at him.

Decklan sighed as the fingers of his other hand began to slip off the rail.

This is what you've always wanted, isn't it you bitch? Fine, have your wish.

Decklan dropped face-first from the side of the Chris Craft into the frigid water below. The alcohol lessened the initial shock of the cold and within seconds, Decklan felt himself sinking below the surface. The current grabbed hold of him, pushing him away from the anchored boat. He looked up and saw at least ten feet between his intended watery tomb and the diminished light of the world above.

Open your mouth and take a deep breath. Finish the job, Decklan. For once in your life, follow through on your responsibilities.

Decklan's lungs began to burn from lack of oxygen. He wanted to kick his legs and arms and flail his way back to the surface but managed to ignore the instinctive panic and force himself to be still.

In the seconds before his death, Decklan Stone had finally found some measure of peace.

I'm ready.

He welcomed the coming darkness.

Planet Earth is blue and there's nothing I can do…
    The writer opened his mouth, breathed as much water in as he possibly could, and ended his life.

18.

Adele returned to the home of Martin and Will Speaks. She moved quickly down the hallway and into Martin's bedroom while holding her cell phone in her right hand.

There they are, the same marks as the picture showed. That freezer has been moved back and forth in the exact same spot over the wood floor hundreds of times.

A section of the floor to the left of the freezer was badly marred where the bottom of the appliance had been slid across the hardwood over the course of many years.

Adele intended to move it yet again. She placed both hands against the freezer's side and gave it a hard shove. It moved just a few inches. She shoved again, and then again, until finally the space that had been hidden behind the freezer was revealed.

It was a small, square door with a deadbolt lock on the outside. Even with the door shut, Adele could smell the fetid aroma of human waste.

As bad as the smell was, Adele had every intention of finding out what had been kept hidden on the other side. She pulled back the deadbolt and opened the door and was immediately assaulted by a gag-inducing stench that was many times more powerful than when the door was closed.

Once she was certain she wouldn't vomit, Adele used her cell phone as a flashlight and stuck it into the space beyond the door. The light illuminated a set of narrow, wood steps leading down into further darkness.

Adele was unable to move beyond the top of the stairs, overcome by fear and revulsion of what she might find waiting for her at the bottom of the steps.

What was that?

Her keen ears picked up a soft, shuffling noise from somewhere in the hellish darkness beyond the stairs. She extended her cell phone light further into the passageway with a badly shaking hand.

Someone, or something, was watching her from below. Adele couldn't see it yet but knew it to be true.

A thump echoed off the bottom step. And then another, and yet another. Whatever was down there was now coming up.

Adele tried to move back, but her legs remained frozen in place. The sound of the approaching footsteps grew closer.

A bone-white human hand shot out from the darkness, encircled Adele's right wrist, and gripped it tightly between dirt-encrusted fingers, causing her to drop the cell phone down into the void below. A thing of nightmare emerged from the inky abyss of the stairwell and glared out at Adele from yellow orbs as thin, scabbed lips drew back in a black-gummed grimace.

They were the eyes of madness housed within the face and body of a monster.

Adele screamed and finally found the strength to fling herself backwards. She fell against the bedroom wall opposite the hidden door with enough force she cracked the sheetrock behind her.

The thing's eyes rolled inside of its tight-skinned skull as it looked around the room and then back to the horrified young woman who stood before it. It wore the remnants of a once-white dress that hung from a few remaining threads off of jagged-boned shoulders. The desiccated legs were covered in mottled and malformed, deep-red scabs, the result of rat bites that took place nightly when the creature managed to fall asleep in a dug-out hole that was its primary place of rest in the cellar below the home.

The thing's jaws unhinged and the mouth opened as a hand extended toward Adele. Two tracks of tears slowly fell from its eyes and then intersected at the bottom of its chin.

"Please…help me."

It was not the voice of a monster, but rather of a woman, frail, frightened, and with just a hint of hope that her many prayers had finally been answered.

Adele heard the undeniable humanity in that voice and knew something of what the woman once was still remained. She pushed aside her fear and revulsion and gently took Calista Stone's hand into her own.

Both women turned at the sound of a vehicle pulling up to the home.

Calista pulled away in a panic and began to scramble back to the stairwell.

"I will help you, Calista," Adele said. "Look at me."

Calista paused but her eyes remained wide and fearful. Adele took a slow, deliberate step toward the woman the world had for so long thought was dead.

"We are walking out of here together—right now."

Calista shook her head and began to back into the cellar door. Adele knew she had to say something or risk both their lives should the Speaks men find them.

"Decklan is waiting for you, Calista. He has been waiting a very long time. I can take you to him, but you have to come with me now."

Calista blinked several times, as if awakening from an especially deep and troubled sleep. She looked down into the darkness beyond the stairs, and then back to Adele. When she spoke, it was a hoarse, hushed whisper.

"I want to see my husband again."

Adele placed her hand around Calista's forearm and guided her toward the back of the house. The sound of the pickup truck grew louder with each step they took. She knew they only had seconds before father and son reached the front door and after that, both Calista and her would have to run as fast as possible down the long driveway and hope they had enough time to reach the road before being caught. She pushed open the plywood backdoor and pulled Calista through into the outside world. On the other side of the house the truck shut off.

"Hurry, Calista. This way!"

Adele moved quickly along the back of the home, and then turned the corner to find Martin and Will Speaks staring at her. They both looked shocked, but that quickly transformed into seething anger. It was then Adele realized her error. She had assumed they used the front door.

"What are you doing with my mother?" Will asked. He stood pointing at Adele with eyes blazing. His jeans and hoodie were soaked with saltwater from trying to stop the leak in his father's boat. Adele drew a sharp breath. She recognized the hoodie from the night in the university library basement, confirming what she had already suspected.

It was him.

"My boy asked you a question, young lady."

Martin Speaks pulled a revolver from an ankle holster and pointed it directly at Adele's chest.

"I'm taking her with me is what I'm doing," Adele replied. "People already know I'm here—*lots* of people."

The former sheriff's eyes narrowed, and then he gave Adele a contemptuous sneer.

"Is that right? Looks to me like a clear case of breaking and entering. I am well within my rights to shoot you dead, and I assure you, that's *exactly* how it'll be written up. My boy tried to warn you. I'm not the kind of man you want to piss off. I knew you talking to the writer was going to be trouble for us. I told you to stay away, and now here you are, messing with things you should have just left alone."

Calista, who was crouched behind Adele, began to make a soft whimpering noise. Adele forced herself to remain calm. She knew if she allowed Martin Speaks to intimidate her, both she and Calista would never leave the property alive.

"I wouldn't count on the local authorities covering for you on this one, Mr. Speaks. Too many people know, including the authorities in Bellingham. You're done. Let me and Calista go. I don't know why you took her, why you've been keeping her, *but it's over.*"

Martin's eyes lit with rage, then regret, and then back to rage. Adele sensed he wanted to shoot her, but then, inexplicably, he lowered his weapon.

Will appeared on the verge of panic. "You won't let her take Mom, right Dad? I can't sleep without knowing Mom is still with us. She helps make m-m-me better. Let's keep them both! There's enough room. We can get another chair. She can be young again, right? We can make Mom young again. We can have old Mom and young Mom at the same time."

Martin's lower lip began to tremble. He was coming to terms with twenty-seven years of a terrible secret in just a few seconds. He looked at Adele with pleading eyes, desperate to be understood. He had been a respected lawman once but the pain of losing his wife and the burden of raising a troubled child proved too much and led to the despicable act of kidnapping Calista and keeping her prisoner.

It had been Will who followed Decklan and Calista Stone from Roche Harbor. And it was Will who overpowered Calista and carried her off the Chris Craft to his father. Will was convinced he had saved Calista from her husband. He told his father that he overheard them arguing, and then how Decklan Stone left his wife alone on the boat. Martin found Calista to be so beautiful, and her remarkable effect upon his son so positive, that he was suddenly willing to do the unthinkable.

It was a secret that bound father and son, but the sheriff suspected it would eventually destroy them both as well. When he suffered the stroke, he raged over having survived it. Twenty-seven years of accumulated guilt had him yearning for death and each day Martin Speaks grew stronger following that stroke, his corrupted spirit was further diminished.

He knew there would be a reckoning one day.

Martin wouldn't allow them to take his son, though. Years ago when Will was struggling terribly in school, Child Protective Services had recommended that he be sent to the asylum on the mainland in nearby Sedro-Woolley. Martin Speaks didn't allow such a thing to happen then, and he was even more determined to not allow it now. Will was his responsibility, and he always would be. If the world had no use for something, you were then required to eliminate that something from the world.

Will placed his hand on his father's shoulder and spoke in tones that clearly indicated confusion, as if the threat of losing Calista was already causing him to revert to his former, more simplistic self. He pointed at Adele.

"I want to keep her, too. She's pretty. I know you said to not even think about it, but now that she's already here—"

Martin suddenly turned, raised the gun to his son's forehead, and fired. Will's body dropped face-first to the ground with the finality of certain death. Martin lowered the gun to his side. He was a man utterly defeated and far beyond any semblance of hope yet still desperate to be understood.

"It just sort of happened," he said. "Will adored Mrs. Stone from the first time he saw her. She was like some New York angel delivered to him. You have to understand that after finding out he was the cause of his mother's death, he was never right. It was the guilt. He was always looking to replace her. He heard them arguing in Roche Harbor and he thought he was helping. He really did."

Martin looked to the brilliant, blue sky and shook his head.

"I thought he'd killed her when I first saw her. Will hit her on the head awful hard. There was blood all over her face. He tied her up, put her on the skiff, and brought her over to Deer Harbor. Then he dumped her in one of those marina carts with the two wheels and spent the rest of the night pushing her all the way back here. He was just so happy when I found him standing outside the house with her bound up in that cart. He was smiling ear to ear. And she *was* beautiful, and I did miss having a woman around here almost as much as Will missed knowing his mother. So, we kept her. It was all easy enough at first. She drowned, her body was never found, and that was that—case closed."

Martin's shoulders slumped and his eyes shut tight as if trying to close a door against the unrelenting onslaught of his deep shame.

"I knew what I did was wrong, but after a few weeks, I had no choice but to keep her here. Do you understand? No choice. And you should have seen what it did for Will. He gained confidence and his speech improved. For the first time in his life, he almost seemed normal. People stopped teasing him so much. I stopped worrying about having to give him up to an institution. For him, she was his mother. But when she kept trying to escape, I decided it best to keep her in the cellar. At first, we brought her out regularly, but then I figured out that Will actually didn't need to see her as much. He just wanted to know she was still down there. So eventually she hardly came out at all. She gave up and accepted her fate. We all did."

Before Adele could stop her, Calista moved toward Will's motionless body, leaned over it and then gently placed her hand on his upper back. Despite the horror done to her over the course of those many years, Calista Stone had enough humanity left to feel the loss of a life that had faced such hardship since its very beginning.

Martin looked down at the woman he had kept prisoner for nearly three decades and began to sob.

"I am so sorry for what we did. I am so sorry for keeping you down there like that all this time."

Just as quickly as Martin's emotional breakdown showed itself, it was pushed aside and replaced by the former sheriff's far more familiar, hard-toned inflection. He straightened his shoulders, lifted his chin upward, and tipped his head to the side.

"You two should be going now."

Calista stood and stared into her longtime captor's hard, flinty eyes, not quite believing he was telling her the truth. Adele needed no such convincing. She grabbed hold of Calista and pulled her toward the driveway that would take them back to the main road.

Martin Speaks didn't bother to watch them go. He no longer cared.

Instead, he dragged the body of his son toward the concrete pad behind the home and then with arms, back and legs straining, lifted his son into one of the three lawn chairs.

"There you go. It's been a long day, hasn't it? A very-very long day."

Martin sat down next to his son, took out a cigarette, and lit it with practiced ease. He inhaled deeply, held the smoke in, and then let it out in a swirling, grey-white nicotine plume. He looked out upon the open expanse of property that had been his family's beginning and end for generations and wondered how things might have been different had Will's mother not died giving birth to him.

He glanced over at his son, noted the already partially coagulated blood oozing from the exit wound in the back of Will's head, and for the first time since before his wife's passing, felt relief.

"I want you to know I tried my best, Will. I also would be the first to admit my best wasn't much to brag about. I wasn't made for raising a child, and you were the evidence of that sad fact. We can both rest now, though. You and me, right out here like we always did. For better or worse, you were my boy."

With the metallic scraping sound of steel against teeth, the former sheriff placed the gun deep into his open mouth, making certain to point it upward toward his brain. If he could have smiled, he would have.

He gave himself a silent countdown.

Three, two, one…

Martin Speaks was finally free.

19.

In death, Decklan Stone finally learned the certainty of heaven. He gazed upon Calista's smiling face and knew all would be well so long as Calista was with him.

He recalled the absolute darkness that quickly followed the water filling his lungs, the brief pain and panic, but remembered nothing after that. And yet, here he was now, looking at the familiar, albeit older, face of his long-dead wife.

She's older. Why is she older?

Decklan became agitated by Calista's appearance. There were deep lines under her eyes and around her mouth where he knew none to be. She was thinner, emaciated in fact.

What kind of heaven would do something like this to someone so beautiful? he thought.

The potential answer to the question caused a lump of panic to form in the writer's throat as he considered the possibility it wasn't heaven he found himself having gone to, but rather the alternative. Decklan shut his eyes and then re-opened them, only to find the same smiling, yet older, and seemingly unhealthier version of Calista looking back at him. He could see her opening her mouth and forming words, but there was no sound. He couldn't hear her.

Decklan was unable to hear anything.

He tried to sit up, but lacked the strength to move, as if a great weight had been placed over his body. A stranger's face moved into Decklan's view to the right of Calista. It was an older man with thinning white hair and glasses. His mouth was moving as well, but like with Calista, Decklan couldn't hear what was being said.

The panic worsened as Decklan thought he was unable to breathe, much like how he felt when he drowned. He tried to scream as he considered that the woman in front of him may not be Calista, but some evil devil who intended to do him harm.

He watched, horrified, as the Calista-thing leaned down close to his face. He could neither hear nor feel her, but rather sensed her closeness.

And then came a sound from a distance seemingly greater than anything Decklan could possibly comprehend. So great, in fact, it was more a suggestion of sound. It repeated itself over and over again until finally, Decklan began to recognize a voice.

It was *her* voice.

Soft, confident, loving.

Calista! his mind cried.

Decklan tried to force his ears to open and allow the sound of that voice to enter his mind more fully. It had been twenty-seven years since he had last heard it.

"It's okay," Calista whispered. "I'm here. I love you, and I'm not going anywhere."

Decklan's eyes were filled by a torrent of grateful tears even as some part of him feared it was all merely a wonderful dream that would be ripped away from him upon waking.

And then he felt something for the first time since his medical resurrection nine days earlier. It was Calista holding his hand inside of her own. He could feel her warmth, realized he had not died, and that by some miraculous intervention, his wife had been returned to him.

Calista moved even closer to her husband and rested the side of her face against his neck. She could feel his pulse, his strength, his life, and was convinced for the first time since watching him for days as he lay unmoving in the hospital bed, that he intended to find his way back to her, however difficult that journey might prove.

To the amazement of the doctor who was still in the room, Decklan Stone somehow found the strength to lift his arms and place them around his wife. And though her husband was not yet able to speak the words out loud, Calista still heard them.

I'm never letting you go.

EPILOGUE

1.

BELLINGHAM UNIVERSITY GAZETTE

The Writer

By Adele Plank

By the time his body was pulled from the cold San Juan waters, the enigmatic figure known by island locals as "The Writer" was very much gone. There was no pulse, no breathing, rather only the absence of life.

Decklan Stone had succeeded in his final wish to be a dead man.

Some who read this might judge him harshly for wanting to take his own life, but such people are among those who willfully possess the insufferable quality of all too quick and generalized judgment. They are more than happy to find fault without knowing the conditions which brought about such a state in a man who from superficial appearances, lived a charmed existence most can only dream of.

Beyond that façade was a man in great pain, faced with having to awaken each time to the fact that it was to be another day without the woman he loved, taken from him in a tragic drowning he thought to be his fault. Eventually, that pain becomes too much, the days too long, the nights far too lonely.

Who among us has not faced a similar misery at some point in our own lives?

And so, the writer decided he had had enough, not knowing that at the very moment he was ending his own life, his long-lost love was being given the opportunity to reclaim her own.

You see, Decklan Stone died just over six months ago, but Calista Stone had been presumed dead for many years. Two deaths intertwined, one very real, one tragically and wrongfully supposed.

I do not wish to make the focus of this article about Calista's time as a prisoner in the cellar of two men who had both descended into madness or of Decklan's time inside a prison constructed of his once seemingly insurmountable guilt. Most, if not all, who are reading this now, will have already been subjected to the names and related news coverage of Martin and Will Speaks. You know of the terrible crime they committed, and the manner in which two lives were nearly destroyed by that act played out over twenty-seven very long years. No, instead I wish to tell you of a shared recovery, for it is recovery that every one of us needs to believe in, and it is recovery that has become the most important aspect of these two remarkable lives.

Mr. Stone spent nearly two weeks in the ICU at Bellingham Medical Center before being moved to more familiar surroundings at the small Friday Harbor rehabilitation center in the San Juan Islands. But for the initial seventy-two hours it took her to partially recover from her own horrifying ordeal, Calista Stone never left her husband's side as they both reacquainted themselves with each other within the resumed blessing that is once again their lives together.

Shortly before Decklan attempted to end his life, he allowed a naïve star-struck fan and aspiring journalist to get a brief glimpse at the real man behind the myth that is the author of *Manitoba*.

He has an undeniably charming presence that is quiet, thoughtful, and with an underlying hint of the humor that I'm certain first drew Calista to him some thirty years ago. He remains confused over the ongoing fuss surrounding his only bestseller. He is not so much humble as he is withdrawn. His desire is to live a simple life of comfortable solitude, keeping distractions at arm's length. He enjoys good wine, strong coffee, and listening to the conversations of others. That is, of course, a common quality of talented writers—the ability to hear, to see, and to observe.

I would be remiss if I did not also admit that he is in this reporter's opinion, a remarkably handsome man. There is an affable mystery to him that draws the eye without any real effort on his part. He exudes a hint of danger that somehow also feels safe, like the hidden cove tucked within the shores of his island home.

When joined with his wife Calista, Decklan Stone is made that much more attractive, for when together, each is truly greater than the sum of their individual parts. Calista's own recovery was both quick and remarkable. Her face softened as she gained weight and strength back, and through the sheer force of her will, she returned herself to the world of the living.

She would later admit to me it was the significant dental work that was necessary to reconstruct her smile that was the worst of all. Apparently being "dead" for so long did nothing to lessen her fear of the dentist. When Decklan complained of the toll his physical rehabilitation was taking on him, it was Calista who demanded he toughen up and to keep pushing himself to improve, regardless of pain and fatigue.

"I lost you for twenty-seven years, Decklan Stone. I'll be damned if I'm going to sacrifice any more time without you!"

Decklan's speech was the most difficult for him to recover. More than once I saw his frustration as his uncooperative tongue slurred the simplest of words, but he would try again. He had enough of giving up.

Interestingly, or perhaps predictably, Decklan never lost his ability to write. When the spoken word failed him, he would take hold of one of the many pens he kept near his hospital bed and write in the most beautiful cursive. It was usually a comment, expression, or observation that was perfectly suited to the moment.

On my first visit he wrote:

I neglected to hold my breath!

Even in the throes of a very difficult rehabilitation brought about by nearly four minutes where his brain went without oxygen as his body slowly drifted underwater, Decklan Stone remained the writer.

The media attention surrounding the events of Mr. Stone's near death, and Mrs. Stone's incomprehensible journey out of that hole that was her world for so long, has been predictably intense. Neither of them has granted an interview with the exception of yours truly. They have indicated they trust me fully and owe me entirely for returning their life to them. It is praise I believe myself unworthy of receiving, and I cannot fully express in words the honor I feel in their having given it.

I have asked Calista if she has any hatred toward the two men who kept her prisoner under their house all those years. She replied that hatred was too strong a word and that sadness would be a more appropriate description. She also stated she never believed she would die in the darkness of that cellar. Calista Stone is the strongest person I will likely ever know, and it was that strength that allowed her to never give up hope that she might one day walk out of that house of horrors a free woman, and most remarkably, with her soul still intact.

She did just that.

I couldn't have done so, and likely neither could you.

The investigation by Washington State authorities was very professional and comprehensive, though, as so often happens when we are confronted by such evil, they never reached a conclusive explanation for why Martin and Will Speaks did what they did. Certainly, the loss of his mother hindered Will's emotional development, but perhaps his limitations would have existed anyway. As for Martin Speaks, the former sheriff of San Juan County, his motivations remain even more difficult to decipher. Was it fear of losing his son? A psychological report dating back to Will's childhood indicates that was a very real possibility. Perhaps the atrocious crime enacted on Calista Stone was the result of genuine, albeit terribly twisted, love for his troubled child.

In the end, however, it was Martin Speaks who allowed Calista Stone to leave. Perhaps in doing so, he secured at least some of the redemption that in the end, he so clearly hoped to find.

The related death of Decklan Stone's longtime island neighbor and Orcas Island store owner, Bella Morris, was ruled a murder, one most likely committed by Will Speaks having tampered with the propane tank line that served Bella's Deer Harbor store. A witness indicated Will had been speaking in a particularly loud and excited manner with Bella earlier that morning and mentioned to her that he was going to get a new mother to replace the other one because she was, "getting too old." He went on to exclaim he would save the new one from the writer just like he did the old one. That in turn led to a phone message Bella left for Decklan Stone, the same message authorities took possession of when I gave them my own recorded version of it. The authorities believe Martin Speaks overheard or perhaps later learned of what his son said to Bella Morris, and then warned him that doing so would result in his mother being taken from him. A confused and frightened Will Speaks then enacted his plan to silence Bella, who, upon arriving at her beloved store that morning, turned on the cooking area stove unaware of the gas that was leaking out as she did so.

My brief time with Bella Stone left me with one certainty regarding the manner of her death—she deserved better.

Recently, I visited the still burned-out husk of Bella's store with Calista Stone. She said nothing to me as we looked over the remains of what had been Bella's later-in-life work. Then Calista gave a knowing smile and declared it would be rebuilt in Bella's honor. She had already spoken of the plan with Decklan. They intend to buy the space, construct a new store, and call it, *Bella's Deer Harbor*. She was especially excited at the prospect of having college kids come to work at the store during the busy summer months and asked me if I might know of anyone at the university who would like to do so.

I told her I most certainly did. I'm looking forward to being one of her first employees, knowing that Calista will make a wonderful boss.

Two weeks after that visit, I returned to the islands for a private service for a man I had come to love and respect during the intense and all too brief time I knew him. Delroy Hicks, longtime and loyal-to-the-end friend of Decklan Stone, passed away from cancer shortly after having helped to save Decklan's life. I wondered if Delroy had always known he needed to remain alive long enough for that very purpose. I wouldn't put it past him. He was a truly remarkable human being. I was told Delroy maintained his wry humor and general fearlessness until the very end. His last few days were spent inside a small room at the Friday Harbor hospital drifting into and out of consciousness. Decklan recalled for me how during the morning before Delroy passed, he took Decklan's hand and squeezed it with his own and then gave him a quick wink. A moment later he asked Decklan if he would, "Fetch me my fedora from the closet, yeah?"

Decklan was happy to oblige him and when he asked Delroy why it was so important that he wear his hat, Delroy grunted and then pulled the brim down low over his eyes and declared, "A gentleman should always wear what suits him and this fedora is as much me as I am it. I was wearing it when Old Jack and I managed to pull you out of the water. If that doesn't qualify it as a good luck hat, I don't know what would!"

As always, there was an undeniable wisdom to Delroy's words. Three hours later, Delroy, still wearing his beloved hat, drifted off to sleep again and never woke up.

Decklan, newly redeemed in the eyes of the island community, spoke at the service, but did not use the occasion as some so often do, to prove himself a man of many words with little meaning, but rather a man of few words and great meaning. He stood up in the little church that overlooks Roche Harbor and spoke in a way befitting the remembrance of someone whose company he no longer had the opportunity to enjoy. It was a struggle for him to form each word so that it could be understood. Initially he didn't want to speak out of embarrassment over the slurring that persisted, despite his great effort to overcome it. It was Calista who reminded her husband of his obligation to Delroy and once that was made clear, Decklan quickly pushed his own embarrassment aside, feeling greater shame for having entertained that embarrassment in the first place.

"I don't have the luxury of calling many my friend," Decklan said that day. "Delroy Hicks was that very thing. If not for him, I would have drowned in my own pain a long time ago. He was a good mentor, a better man, and I hope to live my life in such a way that I truly earn the second chance he gave to me. Goodbye, old friend."

At the conclusion of Delroy's service, a still-living ghost of both Calista's and Decklan's shared past, made her way to them. Roche Harbor hotel owner Tilda Ashland's feelings for Calista, and her long-simmering hatred of Decklan for Calista's supposed death, was, and likely remains, a complicated affair. I don't know what was said between them, but I do know it ended with a long hug between the two women, and a brief handshake between Tilda and Decklan. I can't say for certain if all was forgiven, but it did appear that healing was finally underway.

The now internationally known story of Decklan and Calista's tale of love lost and love found has made Decklan Stone a bestselling author for the second time in his life as sales of *Manitoba* have subsequently skyrocketed. For weeks his publicist urged Decklan to do interviews, book tour signings, and other promotions to more fully take advantage of his newly rediscovered fame.

He finally relented, but true to Decklan's nature, it was on his terms. He did just one book signing at Suzanne Blatt's *Island Books* in Friday Harbor. Decklan's publicist shipped a thousand copies of *Manitoba* to the bookstore for the signing. They sold out in just four hours.

Decklan, still undergoing his physical therapy sessions, sat in a chair behind a small desk and in his quiet, unassuming way, proceeded to sign every copy put in front of him. Calista stood near her husband, protective, beautiful, and dignified. I was amazed by her transformation from the thing that emerged out of that cellar, to the elegant, silver-haired woman who watched over Decklan with glimmering eyes that so clearly communicated the kind of love we would all wish to have in our lives.

When the copies of *Manitoba* ran out, Decklan remained to take photos with fans like Bill Baldwin. Decklan signed Bill's old copy and shook his hand, an act that left the restaurant owner stammering with gratitude. And though Decklan's speech had not fully returned, he was no longer ashamed of his struggle to form words. He didn't have to be. The words that sprung from his mind were more than enough. When a reader told him how much they loved *Manitoba*, Decklan would smile, look directly into their eyes, and tell them thank you in his hushed, slightly slurred voice.

When the last of the fans finally left the bookstore, Decklan Stone stood, turned to Suze and gave her a hug. The bookstore owner was both stunned and deeply grateful for the gesture. I had shared with Decklan that Suze had told me she never believed Decklan was responsible for Calista's death. On that day I was able to see how much those words really meant to him.

Calista then stepped forward with an immaculate, hardcover version of *Manitoba*. She handed it to her husband who then gave it to Suze.

He took a deep breath and then with careful focus, proceeded to say, "First copy, first edition—it's yours."

Suze's mouth fell open. The reaction made Decklan's face light up with a warm smile. He gently gripped the bookstore owner's shoulders and reaffirmed just how much he valued her loyalty.

"Thank you for believing in my better nature."

I remained inside the bookstore with Suze as we both watched Decklan and Calista make their way into the world that awaited them outside. They held hands as they did so, older in years, but still very young in their affection for each other. In a way, they were beginning all over again.

Earlier that morning at their home, I had asked Calista if she regretted the loss of so much time. She sat quietly considering the question and then we both heard the sound of an old typewriter, the very same typewriter upon which *Manitoba* had been forged decades ago. Decklan was writing again, his muse having finally returned to him.

Calista tilted her head and grinned. She clearly enjoyed the sound of her husband at work.

"I would be lying if I said I didn't entertain such regret. But then I consider that, though we lost those twenty-seven years, we're not yet sixty, still relatively young. I'm determined to have more than another twenty-seven years together. I think we're owed that much."

I recall looking across the kitchen table at Calista and seeing her staring at me as she raised and then lowered her coffee cup. The look in her eyes indicated the kind of determined resolve and confidence that would no longer allow anything to be taken from her, particularly something as important as time.

"In fact," she said. "I won't accept a day less."

Decklan and Calista Stone had lost each other once and had no intention of ever doing so again.

That kind of love would have it no other way.

2.

Many years later.

A young family was enjoying their time on the pristine San Juan Islands waters. The small, scuffed, twenty-seven-year-old cruiser was far from the newest or most attractive boat moving about the islands, but it was theirs.

Two children rested on the vinyl bench at the rear of the boat, their heads poking out from orange life jackets like a pair of grinning turtles. The young wife looked up from her book as her husband steered the little cruiser toward the picturesque entrance to Deer Harbor.

The son shouted and pointed to the sky where a pair of eagles flew overhead. It was a summer in the San Juan Islands. Only those who have experienced it can understand its unique gifts.

It is truly a place like no other.

"How's the book?"

The wife glanced at her husband and nodded.

"It's pretty good. Started a little slow, but now I'm hooked."

The husband glanced at the book's cover and noted the title.

Manitoba.

The daughter made her way to the helm and stood between her parents. The girl stared at the small, tree-lined island that served as a natural navigational marker for boats coming into the harbor.

The father could hear his daughter mumbling something but couldn't quite make out the words. He leaned down closer.

"The people on the cliff," she said.

Both he and his wife looked to where their daughter was pointing, and soon their son looked as well.

An older couple was holding hands as they sat in two wooden chairs overlooking one side of their private island. They could easily look down onto the small beach area below and the waters beyond. Several tall evergreen trees rose up behind them. The cliff directly underneath their feet was a combination of sea-darkened sandstone and granite that jutted outward several feet before dropping to the rocky shore below.

"Those two seem pretty happy up there," the wife remarked.

The husband gave a quick nod in agreement. It was an image that made him think of the kind of future he would like to share with his wife, the woman he had fallen so madly in love with, the woman who had made him a father, and ultimately, a better man. He smiled.

"Maybe that'll be us someday."

The young mother looked at her husband with eyes squinting from the bright sun overhead and returned the smile. The sound of seagulls echoed across the harbor and intermingled with the soft, lulling song of the water as it slid down the small boat's hull.

"This would be a great place for you to focus on your writing," she said. "Although, you'll have to sell a lot more books before we could afford a place like that."

Their son started to wave at the couple on the cliff and soon the whole family was doing the same.

Just before the boat moved past the idyllic little island, the old couple lifted their hands in unison and waved back. It was both a gesture of greeting and good-bye as well as a gentle reminder to the young family to appreciate that most precious of all human commodities.

Time.

The San Juan Islands Mysteries continues with book #2, Dark Waters, available now at Amazon.com

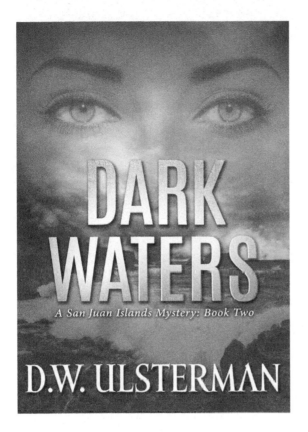

About the Author

D.W. Ulsterman resides in the Pacific Northwest with his wife of thirty years where they are the proud parents of two grown children.

He is the author of multiple bestsellers including The Irish Cowboy and the San Juan Islands Mystery series.

In the summer months he can often be spotted navigating the waters of his beloved San Juan Islands which are the inspiration for many of the stories he writes.

He's also best friends with Dublin the Dobie.

Made in the USA
Las Vegas, NV
29 September 2022

56236233R00134